Shakti Niranjchana is of south Indian origin. She is a graduate of Madras University and presently lives in Canada.

SHAKTI NIRANJCHANA

The Web of Silk and Gold

To

ORRIN SETHER

Dear Orrin,

Wanted you to have my
very first novel, It was
a great pleasure to meet you

affly

Shakti Niranjchana

5th April 2004

PENGUIN BOOKS

Penguin Books India (P) Ltd., 11 Community Centre, Panchsheel Park, New Delhi 110 017, India
Penguin Books Ltd., 80 Strand, London WC2R 0RL, UK
Penguin Group Inc., 375 Hudson Street, New York, NY 10014, USA
Penguin Books Australia Ltd., 250 Camberwell Road, Camberwell, Victoria 3124, Australia
Penguin Books Canada Ltd., 10 Alcorn Avenue, Suite 300, Toronto, Ontario, M4V 3B2, Canada
Penguin Books (NZ) Ltd., Cnr Rosedale & Airborne Roads, Albany, Auckland, New Zealand
Penguin Books (South Africa) (Pty) Ltd., 24 Sturdee Avenue, Rosebank 2196, South Africa

First published by Penguin Books India 2001

This is a work of fiction. Names, characters, places and incidents either are the product of the author's imagination or are used fictitiously, and any resemblance to actual persons, living or dead, events or locales is entirely coincidental.

Typeset in *PalmSprings* by SÜRYA, New Delhi
Printed at Chaman Offset Printers, New Delhi

Thank you. This is your book, not mine.
You wrote it in my heart.

ONE

Months may become years, and years, decades; but the memories of my childhood and youth will always haunt me. Today, after I have escaped to a different land, they still invade the present, like the icy mists that hide the rugged peaks of the Himalayas during winter months. Only now, at a distance, the disparate events smooth into a canvas, like the pieces of a jigsaw settle into a beautiful picture.

I don't remember very much of my early years. The stories often repeated by my mother and aunts made it obvious that my birth was not a joyous occasion for my family. I was the third daughter, and for Indian parents, this was not an event for celebration.

My parents had to live with the sweeping shame of not having a son. Any relatives who visited us always commented on the futility of my father's immense fortune, as there was no male heir to carry on the family name. Amma sighed at the sight of my strapping male cousins.

She felt that she had let Appa down. The births of my two sisters had been shameful enough for her. When she conceived for a third time after a lapse of eight long years, my parents had very different reactions. Amma was afraid of the ridicule she would face if she delivered a third daughter. Appa firmly believed he had fathered a son and saw this pregnancy as the answer to all his prayers.

My father's sister Revathy Athai never tired of telling me the story of the drama that preceded my birth. Many pujas were conducted and baskets of rice and vegetables were given to the poor in the hope of propitiating the gods to ensure that the child would be the much-desired son. My father arranged a meeting with a famous astrologer, a man of over eighty years who left his abode in Kashi only once every/year to travel all over India to meet his devotees. Appa must have paid a fortune to schedule this meeting. Revathy Athai described with relish how she and her sisters dressed my mother in the prescribed crimson silk sari and put a huge black dot on her left cheek. Amma was taken to the astrologer with much ceremony, accompanied by a host of relatives carrying trays of fruits, gold, fine clothing and money.

The astrologer peered closely at my mother's palm. I could imagine her plump soft palm in his skinny wrinkled one. Appa and the relatives hung on each mysterious Sanskrit verse that he uttered. Almost no one understood what he was saying, yet everyone assumed that it was something special and divine. Finally he declared: 'She will have a son!' Happiness rippled through the waiting crowd. Amma blushed. Egged on by the enthusiasm his words aroused, the astrologer went on to say that her eyes, the shape of her belly, and the pallor of her face indicated that the boy would be very handsome and successful. Appa was triumphant, the one blemish in his existence was rectified.

I squashed all this enthusiasm, belied the astrologer's expensive prediction, and shattered my father's pride and my mother's hopes when I arrived six months later, most definitely a girl. My mother cried for days after I was born. My naming ceremony was very simple and only a few people were invited. They placed me in the same carved sandalwood cradle that my sisters had once lain in and rocked me while the women sang devotional songs. Amma later told me that I looked very beautiful as I lay staring up at the brilliant green parrot-shaped mobiles they had hung over me. The priest, whose responsibility it was to decide what letter the infant's name should begin with, came up with the letter 'A' for my name. They almost named me Abirami after my father's mother, but my youngest aunt insisted that it was too old-fashioned, and so I became Aradhana. Amma said that Aradhana was the name she had wanted me to have.

I spent the first eighteen years of my life in Madurai. When I think back, I can feel the heat and the dust of that city climb into my nostrils and awaken my memory. I remember it as a huge noisy place with narrow roads, always packed with vehicles and buzzing with activity. Lorries overloaded with hay and bricks forced their way through the ranks of squealing auto-rickshaws, bicycles were piled with children, and buses spilled over with passengers. Vending carts lined the roads, loaded with bug-infested fruits, sweetmeats and snacks, their owners screaming at the top of their lungs to be heard above the cacophony of blaring horns. Amidst all this chaos, the ancient traffic of bullock carts continued as it had for centuries. The bullocks, mercilessly beaten by their drivers, looked pitiable with the taut ropes pulling at their gaping nostrils and their rubbery tongues trying in vain to disperse the cheerful flies that swarmed around them. Pedestrians tried to make their way through the traffic, cursing the vehicles and vendors. Occasionally, there would be a silver Mercedes, inching along in the crowded street, the chauffeur's brow furrowed as its imported glory was clouded by domestic dust. And sometimes a temple elephant would saunter along, stretching its fleshy trunk into cars to gather alms.

The Meenakshi Amman temple with its four great gopurams stretching skywards was the pride of Madurai. It was the tallest building in the city, as old as the city itself. People believed that if they constructed a building taller than the temple gopurams, they would incur the wrath of the gods. It was a spectacle of artistic flamboyance, crafted entirely of stone and filled with exquisite detail. The dark narrow hallways with their dank moist floors were always crowded with devotees and beggars, and filled me with awe and fear. I can still smell the flowers and burning incense, a fragrance as permanent as the grey walls themselves. Every day hundreds of worshippers came to seek the blessing of the goddess. The Western tourists with expensive cameras and cotton shorts and T-shirts made quite a contrast to the elaborately dressed Indian devotees. During the puja, men removed their shirts and threw themselves on the ground in supplication before the statue of Meenakshi. Today, it amuses me to picture all those men, who probably mistreated their wives, grovelling before the image of a female deity.

I grew up in a sheltered household, the wealth of my parents insulating me from the struggles of life. I was untouched by poverty and ignorant of the hardships amidst which most people lived. I was always a lonely child because of the huge age difference between my sisters and me. Our house was like a palace, rambling and beautiful, set in half an acre of fertile land. My father had not stinted on anything when he built this house. He had hired a very expensive architect. The elaborate woodwork in its interiors had probably decimated a small forest. The floors were made of milk-white marble imported from Italy. From the Jaipur vases to the Kashmiri carpets and the handcrafted tables, it was like a museum to display my father's wealth. There were a lot of servants always scurrying around. I had my own personal maidservant; she was a child herself.

My most vivid memory of my childhood is sitting on the huge sandalwood swing in the porch and rocking myself to dreamland. I can close my eyes even today and hear the sound of the creaking hinges. It was from this vantage position that I would spend hours gazing at the dusty road and the numerous people walking in the boiling heat. This was the only time that I got a glimpse of the world outside my father's mansion, and I realized early in life that outside our huge gates there existed quite a different world. I looked with wonder at the ill-clad women, men and children, who sometimes peered with longing into my garden and my house. The children especially, gazed curiously at my dolls and my expensive clothes as I sat on that sweet-smelling swing.

Our house was air-conditioned and I rarely went out in the heat, so I did not even know how it was to feel the hot sun on my head though I lived in a city where the temperature was an easy forty-five degrees centigrade. I was driven to wherever I had to go in air-conditioned cars. Appa did not allow us to use public transport, not even the school bus. He wanted his daughters to grow up without the influence of outsiders, especially men. Appa's enormous donations to the school ensured that the teachers gave us special privileges. There were laboratories and blocks of classrooms bearing his name on a plaque. The very name Krishnamoorthy Nadar was enough to create a stir in a crowd. He owned numerous theatres and restaurants. He was also very influential with the government. Ministers and members of parliament frequented our house. I remember looking wide-eyed at the huge train of cars bearing men clad in white landing often at our doorstep. Even the commissioner of police was at Appa's beck and call. From a very early age I was aware of the power and clout my family enjoyed. It was difficult to ignore it.

Apart from the hours at school, I spent most of my time in my room, playing make-believe games. The only people I saw were my family. But I did not spend very much time with them either. My mother did not read me bedtime stories and my father never kissed me goodnight. Amma was always in the house so I could trail after her when I wanted, but Appa was totally removed from the sphere of my existence. He was the provider who ensured that I lived in ease and luxury, and so the most important person in the house and in our world. But to me, he was a remote figure who seldom spoke to me. We did not see him in the mornings. By the time we got ready for school and came downstairs, he was already gone. In the evenings, we would be in bed by the time he returned. Even if he got back while we were still up, Appa ate separately. I remember sneaking down the stairs and secretly looking at him while Amma served him dinner. He looked very powerful and I felt proud looking at him. Of course I loved him, but I feared him more. My father took his patriarchal role very seriously. This meant that I never rode piggyback on his shoulders or sat on his lap. I had seen cousins being hugged by their fathers and I badly wanted Appa to cuddle me and kiss me. That never happened. The most affectionate gestures were the occasional pats he gave me. I loved the feel of his big strong hand on me.

Appa's word was law in every aspect of our lives. No one could dream of questioning his dictates. Amma believed that her prime duty was to serve Appa. I have never seen my parents sitting together and talking. Except for soft-toned affirmations, I don't remember Amma ever having a conversation with my father. Today I wonder whether she ever expressed her own opinions and desires to her own husband.

The only family outings we had were when Appa took us to the Meenakshi temple on Sundays. My first memories of going to the temple are from when I was five or six. I enjoyed this weekly outing and all the rituals associated with it. My two sisters, then in their early teens, would dress in long pleated silk skirts in brilliant colours. Amma would call them to her room and open the huge wooden almirah. Out would come her hand-carved jewellery box lined with red velvet cloth and she would carefully adorn my sisters with gold. I would watch with awe and envy, for they looked like ethereal goddesses. I was only a child, too young for silk and gold. Amma would dress me in an imported frock embellished with roses and satin bows. I felt like a princess. For Amma, dressing me in frocks was a matter of pride. In our Nadar community, people displayed their wealth through their clothes and jewellery. Married women especially, were expected to wear as much jewellery as possible to flaunt their husbands' affluence. So on Sundays, after we children were dressed, Amma would appear in a gorgeous silk sari and fabulous jewellery. We would then file into Appa's car and proceed to the temple.

I loved the smell of camphor and incense in the temple. But I was frightened by the disproportionately large breasts and hips of the goddesses. To my child-eyes, they did not have much religicus appeal. I would stare at my father as he diligently performed his religious duties. Appa was a very orthodox and devout Hindu. The temple authorities loved him for his huge donations to the temple funds. On seeing our family, the priests would rush to serve us. The archanai usually lasted for an hour. I would sometimes get distracted in the middle of it. At such moments, Appa would frown at me. That was sufficient to put me back on my best behaviour.

We rarely socialized with anybody other than close relatives. Because of our wealth my parents were always concerned about the evil eye. This kept them wary of less prosperous relatives and friends. My mother spent a lot of money buying various lucky charms and stringing them around the house. There was always a fresh green pumpkin sliced and splayed with red powder grinning at our doorstep to ward off evil. Many things were taboo for Amma. She tied black threads on our wrists and rarely let us out of her sight. I was not allowed to go and play with the neighbourhood children. I spent my evening hours peering through the huge glass window in the hallway at the children playing kabaddi outside, their bare feet kissing the rising dust. The sound of their laughter and chatter filled me with a rush of longing to go and join that lively crowd. Occasionally I pleaded with my mother to let me go out and play. Amma cautioned me severely and warned me of the many infections I would catch by mingling with the other children. The only times I played with other children was when I was in school. At home, I spent my time creating imaginary friends.

Amma was frightened of poor people. She was very charitable, but whenever she was accosted by beggars, she was terrified. She would quickly summon the housekeeper and ask her to send away the beggars after giving them a few rupees and some rice. As a child, I shared her apprehension and thought beggars were mad or strange creatures, not quite human.

I attended the same all-girls' school as my sisters. Even the teaching staff was all women. I loved school because it was my first and only contact with the outside world. I made a lot of friends there. One of them was Lauren. I think I liked her instantly because of her name, which was different from the names I was used to. Her parents were Anglo-Indian. Lauren's father was a handsome man with pale skin and grey eyes. He would come every evening in his little blue car to pick her up. One day, he lifted her high up into the air when she came running to meet him, his face lighting up with pleasure. I stood there, watching wide-eyed and chewing curiously on the cloth handle of my schoolbag, wondering if my father would do that to me if I asked him. That evening I waited eagerly for my father to return. When he came in, I rushed up to him and gave him a bear hug.

'Appa,' I said, 'will you please toss me up?'

My father looked surprised and somewhat embarrassed. He pushed me away gently.

'Aradhana,' my mother said, 'don't trouble Appa.'

I felt sad. I did not want to trouble him. Much as I enjoyed Amma's soft caresses, I longed for Appa's strong embraces. I think I realized that day that my father would never display his affection for me. I went upstairs to my room in silence and curled up beneath my pink-and-white blanket. I wondered if my sisters ever felt the same way about him. They generally avoided him, largely out of fear and awe.

We were taught early in life that men had to be treated with special respect. I often envied the preferential treatment my male cousins received at all family gatherings. We girls grew up knowing that the central event in our lives was one over which we had no control;

that one day we would have to marry a stranger whom our parents would select for us, and whom we would have to treat with awe and reverence too. Our upbringing was geared towards this. I remember the cooking classes my sisters had when they were in their early teens. It began with the simplest dishes, Amma spending days teaching them how to make perfect fluffy rice. Once this was mastered, they moved on to dishes of increasing complexity. Being able to cook well was mandatory for all women, an essential prerequisite of marriage. It was all training for that ultimate moment in a woman's life: her marriage. Weddings were huge affairs in my community. People often spent their lifetime's earnings on them. They were all arranged marriages and generally the bride did not have any say in the matter.

The first wedding in my family was that of my eldest sister, Neela. She was a very beautiful girl, nine years older than me. When she turned eighteen, Amma started talking about the need to find a husband for her. She thought that Neela should get married soon because only young girls with flexible minds could get accustomed to the traditions of their husband's family.

The old family astrologer Parasuram, whom my parents revered, was summoned. He was a short man with a round face and a rounder belly, always clad in an immaculate white dhoti, with a lot of jewellery and a red, yellow and white tilak on his forehead. He had a round bulbous nose that sat at a rather odd angle above his discoloured smile. His mouth was always stuffed with paan, which he regularly spat out with a loud disgusting noise. To me he looked like an unwashed clown trying to play a serious role.

My parents gave Parasuram Neela's horoscope and astrological charts. Many emotions flitted across his face as he scanned them. My parents peered into his chubby face as if Neela's fate was written on it. After about fifteen minutes, he looked up, a broad grin bridging his cheeks.

'It is a good chart. She will get a good match.' His voice was surprisingly thin and squeaky compared to his form. Appa whispered something to Amma. She immediately went to her room. I heard the iron safe creak as she opened it. She returned with a wad of crisp hundred-rupee notes, which Appa promptly pressed into Parasuram's hands. His grin now seemed to meet his ears.

In the months that followed, Parasuram often visited our house, carrying with him a list of prospective grooms. Finally one day my mother beckoned to me, a huge smile on her face. She held a photograph.

'Aradhana,' she said, 'this is your future brother-in-law, Shivakumar.'

I stared eagerly at the picture. He had a rather broad face and luminous eyes, and a moustache sat smugly above his upper lip. He resembled a local movie star. I liked the look of him, and the prospect of a brother-in-law was exciting. I followed Amma upstairs as she went to show the photograph to Neela. Neela viewed it glumly. I could not tell if she was happy or sad.

'Do you like him?' Amma asked.

'Is he tall?' Neela responded in her gentle voice.

'Well, he is rich and he is educated. He is a nice boy,

a doctor. He and his family live in Tripura. Appa has set his heart on this match. You should not disappoint him. When they come here to fix the wedding, I want you to be on your best behaviour.'

Neela looked at her with wide, rather scared eyes.

After Amma left the room, I snuggled close to Neela. I loved to do this, because she always smelt so good, and to play with the many tinkling bangles she wore on her slender arms. 'Neela,' I said, 'you will have to go away to Tripura after your wedding. Aren't you excited?'

She looked at me strangely. 'I am afraid,' she said. 'I don't want to get married to anybody.'

'But you have to,' I said. 'Anyway, marriage is a lot of fun. They will dress you up in costly saris.' I had attended several weddings with my mother and seen many well-dressed brides. I thought that Neela was very lucky that her turn to play bride had come. I could not understand the reason for her fear.

'Oh, marriage is a sad thing for the bride,' she said abruptly, her eyes welling with tears.

I did not understand. But her words would haunt me for a long time to come.

The following Friday, Shivakumar and his family arrived in two imported cars. Appa went out to greet them. I ran ahead, trying to get my first glimpse of the groom. I saw that he was tall, and so I was content. Neela would be happy now. After all, she had wanted a tall husband. Appa led in his prospective son-in-law with pride.

After they sat down in the living room, Neela came downstairs. I still remember how beautiful she looked in her pale pink sari, a faint blush tinting her cheeks. I looked at Shivakumar. He was staring at her, obviously bowled over. I clasped Neela's palm as she sat in the chair placed especially for her. It was icy cold in the warmth of my own. I felt a surge of affection for her and wished I knew of a way to comfort her.

Shivakumar's mother came over to Neela. Neela bent down and touched the older woman's feet. Shivakumar's mother was pleased.

'You can now go to your room,' she said.

I went upstairs with Neela. 'Did you like Shivakumar?' I asked.

She smiled shyly.

Her wedding was fabulous. Appa spent a fortune. I had never seen such a lavish function before. The house was elaborately decorated, and the pantry stocked with the most delicious and expensive foods. The many rituals began weeks before the wedding. Neela was treated with special honour. The wedding day itself was perfect. Everything went off like a well-performed piece of music. Everyone in Madurai was talking about the wedding for months afterwards.

Neela was going to go away to her husband's home in Tripura three days after the wedding. Amma diligently packed her many suitcases. A truck full of expensive things had already been sent to Agartala. The day before she left, I went to her room and hugged her tight.

She took me in her soft embrace. 'Aradhana,' she said, 'you must be a good girl. I will write to you regularly, and you must write to me.'

I looked up at her face. The prospect of getting real

letters in the mail seemed good. At the age of nine I had rarely, if ever, received letters. Receiving and writing letters made me feel grown-up and important. I temporarily forgot my grief that Neela was going away. I put my head down on her lap and she gently caressed my hair. Just then, Shivakumar entered the room. I hastily got up. He held my palms in his firm clasp and peered into my frightened face.

'Aradhana, don't run away. You are really worried about your sister, aren't you?' He patted my cheek affectionately. 'Don't worry, I'll take good care of her.' He looked at Neela over my head and she blushed faintly. He did seem like a good person. Perhaps he would make my sister happy. I felt strangely better.

'When will you bring her back?' I asked.

'For Deepavali,' he said.

'But that is a long way away!' It was only January and Deepavali was not until November. I wanted to see my sister sooner than that. I looked at him imploringly.

He smothered a laugh. 'Now, Aradhana,' he said, 'I need time to gather all the lovely presents I am going to bring for you when we come to see you. Remember that, and Deepavali will be here before you know it.' That seemed like a satisfactory explanation.

The next morning we bid goodbye to Neela. Amma sobbed into the pallav of her sari. Maya, my second sister, tried to smother her sobs while I cried loudly and unashamedly. Even Appa cleared his throat rather frequently. I could see that he was moved. But Neela did not cry. She did not smile either. She quietly followed her husband into his scarlet van and waved goodbye.

After they left, I slowly climbed upstairs and went into her room. Her perfume still lingered there. On her bedside table, where her photograph as a schoolgirl had earlier stood, there was now a new ivory-framed picture of her and Shivakumar on their wedding day. I picked it up and looked closely at it. Shivakumar had a broad grin on his face and Neela, a shy smile on hers. His proprietorial arm around her shoulder seemed to say that Neela now belonged to him. I got into Neela's bed and snuggled beneath the covers. My tears slowly started to dampen the pillow.

TWO

I missed Neela terribly after she left. Though the difference in age between us was too great for us to be close friends, she had always been gentle and caring. My relationship with Maya was not quite the same. My mother thought that Maya was too clever for a girl. She excelled in quiz competitions and sports, and spent hours solving mathematical equations and doing science experiments. She brought home numerous trophies from school. In an orthodox family like ours, girls were expected to learn to sing bhajans from a very early age and to conduct pujas in their own homes. Maya refused to learn how to do either or to show any interest in cookery and other mandatory girl topics.

She was a rebel in other ways too. She would secretly visit beauty parlours to have her eyebrows shaped. She also had a selection of mini skirts and skin-tight blouses, purchased with her pocket money, which she would model for me. Once when her friend Ramola came to visit her, I saw them steal Appa's cigarettes and take anxious puffs. Maya told my parents that she would go away to America after getting her medical degree, and that she would become a brain surgeon. Even Appa did not try to challenge her. As she grew older, she would engage in debate with Appa on a wide array of topics, ranging from politics to the stock market, and I would watch with awe as Maya dominated these arguments. She treated Appa's discomfiture—revealed in his frequent admonishments that it did not befit women to be too intellectual—with disregard. She considered people who thought of her intelligence as fatal, to be grossly insecure and inferior. Her logical brain had no room for the inadequacies of narrow-minded people.

Though Maya was just a year younger than Neela, nobody pressurized her to get married. My parents would discuss her in hushed tones. Amma complained every day about the great problem that was Maya. Appa believed that once he found a groom for her she would become normal. But I doubted that. I think Appa, too, doubted his own words. He knew that soon after her final exams, Maya would ask him to send her to medical school. He just put off the problem by denying it. Maybe he believed that he could force her to give up her dreams. But this hope was doomed because if ever there was a determined girl, it was Maya. Had she wanted to land on Mars, I am sure she would have done it. She did not let my parents' speculations affect her. She anxiously counted off each day of the three months that remained before she would start medical school.

I thought of Neela often. The house seemed so empty

without her. I waited eagerly for her letters. Then finally one day, the mailman brought a big green envelope with my name inscribed in Neela's neat hand. This was the first of many letters my sister would write to me. She described her life with her new family in great detail, and spoke of her husband with affection and regard. Amma was happy with these letters.

One day Neela called, and Amma was almost incoherent with delight as she spoke to her. Neela had conceived. Amma started chanting the names of her numerous deities in thanksgiving. She swept me up in a hug. 'Neela is going to have a child! I am going to have a grandson!' I did not know how my mother knew it would be a male child. I did not ask her.

Amma disappeared into the puja room, her refuge and sanctuary, and I peeped in to see her muttering fervently before her assembled gods. It was a beautiful room, the floor was inlaid with pink Jaipur marble, and the air was always perfumed with incense. The door was made of sandalwood from Tanjore, carved with twenty-four little elephants whose tusks were fashioned out of real ivory. Beneath each elephant was a crescent-shaped opening in which hung a brass bell that was always polished to perfection. When the door was opened, all the twenty-four bells chimed simultaneously, creating a divine melody to entice the gods. The gods sat with fixed expressions on their little thrones, presided over by the three-headed Brahma. There was also Shiva, Muruga, Ganesha, Hanuman, Krishna, Saraswati and Laxmi, all dressed in fancy jewellery and gaudy clothes. There was also a picture of Jesus, looking rather impoverished among his glitzy colleagues. Amma tended the puja room meticulously. Every day it was washed with clean water from a special copper sembu kudam, after which Amma drew a new colourful kolam on the floor with special multicoloured powder. She adorned these kolams with clay lamps pregnant with castor oil and bearing glowing wicks. The gods were cleaned with a soft silk cloth and adorned with fresh garlands of yellow samanthipoo, white mallipoo and orange kanagambarapoo flowers. The huge brass lamps were kept burning all day so that the room always shone with a golden glow.

When Amma finally emerged from the puja room, she called my father at work. Appa was elated too. Amma spent the rest of the day distributing sweets to the entire neighbourhood. She asked the cook to prepare a selection of pickled vegetables and sweetmeats to send Neela. Other relatives were called and the whole family rejoiced. I found it hard to believe that Neela was going to have her own baby, but I was thrilled nevertheless. Maya was the only one who was concerned.

'Amma,' she said to my mother, 'I think it's too soon. Neela is very young.'

Amma was furious. 'Maya,' she said, 'I had Neela when I was thirteen. And don't talk like that.' Maya shrugged her shoulders and walked off. No criticism ever touched Maya. In our traditional household, she was the free spirit.

My parents decided we should visit Neela in Tripura. Maya had exams coming up and she did not accompany us. I was anxious to see Neela. I wondered if she would look different. I had seen many pregnant women, all of whom had enormous bellies. I thought Neela would have one too. But to my surprise, when I saw her she looked the same, only perhaps a little more fragile. I peered at her stomach and I could see nothing different. It was still as flat as a washboard.

She was as gentle and loving as ever and asked me lots of questions about my life at home and school. She always made me feel important. I loved her for that. In the three days we spent at her home I realized that she truly loved Shivakumar and enjoyed married life. Every evening before he returned from work, she bathed, dressed in a beautiful sari and wore a long strand of fragrant jasmine in her hair. Shivakumar's face would light up on seeing her. They looked just like Sita and Rama from the film of the Ramayana that we saw every Deepavali. The tinkle of Neela's anklets and the sound of her bangles filled the house. Even Shivakumar's family loved Neela for she was kind, docile and caring. I was sad on the day we left. I wished we could spirit Neela away with us. But she seemed so happy in her new life that I said goodbye cheerfully too.

My mother was very pleased with our time in Tripura. Her eldest daughter was married, pregnant and contented. She could want nothing more. In my community, a daughter's first pregnancy was always a prestige issue for her parents as it proved that she was healthy and capable of producing heirs. In that regard, Neela had fulfilled her responsibility, and this made my parents very glad.

Neela was in the seventh month of her pregnancy at Deepavali. Maya had by then gone off to medical college in Chennai. Nobody tried to confront her or stop her. My parents and I went to Agartala for the bangle ceremony for Neela, which in our community is traditionally conducted by the woman's parents in the seventh month of her pregnancy in her husband's home. This is a beautiful ceremony, during which all the womenfolk put multicoloured bangles on the wrists of the mother-to-be. This is meant to make her feel happy and loved, as a happy woman is supposed to deliver healthy and handsome sons. There is also singing and dancing, and an elaborately cooked meal. After this ceremony, as was customary, Neela would stay in our house until after the child was born.

Neela had a round belly now, and looked weighed down by it. Her face was a bit pale. But my mother stated that this was 'normal'. Amma always considered herself as the ultimate authority on everything to do with her daughters. They dressed Neela in a heavy purple and green silk sari inlaid with eighteen-carat-gold zari work. She sat on the floor in the centre of the living room, as was the custom, while all the women smeared dollops of turmeric and sandalwood paste on her wan cheeks. Then they brought out twenty-one plates of different dishes made out of the finest basmati rice. There was yellow lemon rice, white curd rice, red tomato rice, multicoloured vegetable pulao, sweet pongal and a lot of others. She had to eat at least a spoonful of each type, and I could see that she was getting very full. Later we all sat down to partake of the food. All the women were given a set of shiny new glass bangles. I got a dozen bright pink ones set with rhinestones. I immediately adorned my wrists with them and jingled them till the air around me chimed with the sound they made.

Neela bid a tearful farewell to Shivakumar. The finely-spun web of tradition that determined all actions in our family stated that he could not accompany us immediately. I was happy that Neela was coming home with us. The month that followed her arrival was blissful. As Maya was away, Neela spent all her time with me. She told me delightful stories of her life in Tripura. Though I was little more than a child, I could perceive the deep love she shared with Shivakumar. Every night, when she settled into bed, her eyes would fill with tears. I did not ask her, but I knew that she missed her husband.

Just when everything seemed to be going smoothly, the unforeseen happened. One weekend, Shivakumar came down to see Neela. They spent a couple of quiet days together. And on Monday, he left to catch a flight to Agartala. Neela watched his car drive away with tear-filled eyes. A few hours later, they brought his body home in a white ambulance. There had been an accident and he had died instantly.

My mother quickly took Neela to her room and locked the door. I could hear her strangled sobs but I was not allowed to go near her. The house turned still. Relatives filed in at irregular intervals. Everybody talked in hushed tones. Amma suddenly ran out of Neela's room sobbing and told Appa that Neela had started to bleed. I tried to ask Amma what was happening, but she pushed me aside roughly. I was panic-stricken and helpless. I desperately wished that Maya was home. She would have explained what was happening, and she would have known the right thing to do. Within minutes my parents drove Neela to the hospital. I sat at the top of the staircase sobbing silently, clutching my teddy-bear. I must have fallen asleep right there.

When I awoke, it was morning and the marble of the stairs felt very cold. Through the big window in the hall, I could see my father's car parked in the portico. I went downstairs to find my mother. She told me that Neela had lost her baby. An aunt said, 'Just as well. It was a girl anyway.' I wondered if my mother and aunts would have said the same of me, had I died in infancy. That thought made me very unhappy.

Neela was confined to her room for ten days after that. Nobody used her name any more; they just referred to her as 'the widow'. I don't remember the funeral very clearly; it was too sombre for memories. But I do remember my sense of shock when Neela finally emerged from her room that day. She looked like a ghost of her usual radiant self. They had dressed her in an ugly white sari and pulled back her hair into a tight bun. Her ears, arms and neck were bereft of ornaments.

Neela changed completely after that. She stopped smiling and talking. We no longer sat together and chatted for long hours. When I tried to talk to her, she would gently tell me to go and play with my dolls. I wondered why she did not want me near her any more. She confined herself to her room most of the time. Custom dictated that she would stay with us for three months before finally leaving for Shivakumar's home. Sometimes she would accompany my mother to the temple. It was as though all of a sudden she had become a different person.

Our whole family changed too. For months my mother cried every day about the sad misfortune that had befallen the family. My father smoked a million cigarettes to assuage his grief.

After three months, Neela's in-laws came to take her back. As she was leaving with the grim-faced family, she looked up imploringly at my mother. I wanted my mother to tell her to stay with us. But Amma would never violate tradition. I still remember the stricken look on Neela's face as she departed as a widow, for Tripura. The memory of her leaving less than a year ago as a rosy bride clashed jarringly with this. I wondered how Neela would manage there now that there was no Shivakumar to shield her with his love; and his family, for some obscure reason, blamed her solely for his death. Her mother-in-law had called Neela the 'inauspicious one' in our hearing. How would it be when she was alone and helpless?

Neela seldom wrote after this. But we heard that she was not allowed to come out on festivals, and that married relatives avoided her. It was as though she had become a living dead person. The day they lit Shivakumar's corpse on the pyre, they also burnt her self-esteem, her happiness and her youth. I hated the manner in which everyone blamed her for her husband's death. There was something so final about Neela's tragedy.

Some two years after this, when I was twelve, Neela was sent to our house for a month. Her youngest sister-in-law was getting married, and her in-laws did not want the widowed Neela's presence to blemish their auspicious occasion. I felt sorry to see the tired wan creature she had become. Even Amma treated her differently. Not that she mistreated Neela, but she refused to recognize that Neela was still so very young. She was always dressed in a white sari and she was prohibited from adorning herself with jewellery or flowers, which were considered very auspicious for girls and women to wear.

On Fridays, we always bought jasmine to wear after the puja. Neela would look longingly at these flowers and touch them gingerly. I knew that widows were not supposed to wear flowers but then Neela was so young. One Friday, my parents had gone to Thiruthani for a wedding. I preferred to stay back to keep Neela company. She too seemed happy at being left alone with me. The flower girl Thulasi brought flowers to our house as usual. As I paid her and took the flowers, I saw Neela peering at me from the veranda where she was drying her hair in the sun. She looked so beautiful that suddenly I wanted to adorn her hair with the flowers and dress her up in colourful clothes. I ran upstairs to her room.

'Neela,' I said nervously. 'The others won't be here until Monday. Why don't you wear these flowers and your red sari?'

She looked at me oddly. 'Aradhana, you should not talk like that. My husband is dead so I will wear only white.'

'Where is he, Neela?' I asked.

She looked up at the sky with wistful eyes. 'He is in heaven, Aradhana. He is with God.'

I held her soft hands in mine. 'Neela, do you remember how you used to dress up in the evenings for Shivakumar? Don't you think that he will be happy to see you dressed beautifully? Maybe he can even see you from heaven.'

Neela smiled faintly. 'No, Aradhana, that is not appropriate,' she said, caressing my head fondly.

Later that night, as we sat together eating curd rice and mango pickle, Neela looked at me and said, 'You know, Aradhana, just the day before he died, Shivakumar bought me a new sari. He told me that I was to wear it to the temple with him after he returned. He never got back and I never wore it. It just never happened.'

'Show me that sari,' I said.

After dinner she took me to her room. I loved her room. It always smelled of sandalwood, just like Neela. In happier times before her marriage, I used to sit on the soft bed every evening and watch her as she dressed in front of the huge mirror. It all seemed so long ago, so far away. Neela came to me with the sari he had given her. It was a lovely blue with a temple design inlaid with gold zari. I could well imagine the joy with which she and Shivakumar had bought it together. Suddenly she said, 'Let me put it away, Aradhana.' She took the sari from me. I could sense the pain it caused her to see the sari again. After all it had taken her two whole years to talk about it. We did not do much the remaining two days before our parents came back. And after they returned, we did not talk about the sari again. Soon her visit was over and she sadly left for her husband's home.

As I grew up, I saw my sister turn from a vivacious woman, full of joy, to a lonely recluse. Her lovely smile disappeared from her face and the light died in her eyes. No one questioned the life sentence thrust upon her. All she did was pray for the departed soul of her husband. Sometimes I saw her stare into her wedding albums with a strange and wistful look on her face. Much later in life, I realized the intensity of her suffering. In our culture, widowhood is a peculiar and malevolent thing. As a child, I had seen many widows, relatives or friends of my family. I thought of them as an odd species of ill-clothed women with stricken looks. It was only after Neela's widowhood that I realized that they were just ordinary women who had suffered intensely from having been forced to live unnatural lives.

Slowly my family stopped talking about Neela's misfortune. We just accepted it. Amma would go over to Tripura every few months to visit her. She could do nothing more. I used to wonder how my mother had the heart to wear colourful clothes when Neela was forever in white.

THREE

Summer was a special season in my childhood. Schools were closed for the annual break and Madurai was very hot. Our family rested in the air-conditioned comfort of our home; everyone was reluctant to go outside. The ten coconut trees surrounding the house would be pregnant with fruit. Servants would be busy making brooms out of the dried coconut leaves. All day long I would hear the rasp of their little knives as they split the leaves and separated the slender firm veins to make broomsticks. The streets would be filled with wooden carts carrying mounds of red watermelon and yellow musk melon. The 'nongu man', as we called him, would come to sell another summer favourite: the secret hearts of palm fruit. Amma made sure our larder was filled with these natural coolants.

Our household was busiest in summer. The kitchen would buzz with maids attacking mounds of mango and lime to make pickles. The fishmonger Chinnamani's wife was summoned to bring the biggest fish available. I would peer in amazement at the huge heads of fish lying in her basket. Amma would buy the entire basketful, and give her a bowl of rice with fresh sambhar for cutting up the fish into huge chunks, applying turmeric, salt and chilli powder on them and stringing them on a rope to dry them in the sun. Amma gave the dhobi's daughter one rupee and lunch to sit and shoo the crows off the stringed fish. I hated the smell of drying fish, but when the monsoon came, Amma made the most delicious curry with it. Amma was a prudent housekeeper. By the end of summer she would have at least three gunny bags full of dried fish ready for the rest of the year. In summer, Amma also made vadams and papads. She boiled rice with spices and chillies, and patted them onto sheets of polythene to dry in the sun. When they were dry, they would be fried to make the tastiest of snacks. I remember these smells of summer vividly.

During these months, Amma was very lenient with us. I would get up later than usual and eat breakfast before bathing. There were always soft white idlis, with coconut chutney spiced with chillies, and orange sweet kesari swimming in ghee. Amma was especially careful about our health and made us bathe in water boiled with neem leaves. She would grind mehendi leaves and trace delicate patterns on our palms and the soles of our feet to ensure that our bodies remain cool. I remember sitting for hours with the green paste set in designs on my palms. I would ask Amma to scratch my head for me if it itched, so as not to smudge the mehendi on my palms. When the paste was dry, we would rinse it off to reveal bright red patterns on the skin. I loved the brightly coloured designs. Even today, mehendi reminds me of my mother and summer.

Summer was also the season of kites. I would go to the terrace and stare at the sky mottled with multicoloured kites. I often tried to make paper kites, but my kites never flew like the rest. I would then sulk in a corner while my sisters teased, 'Aradhana has made a walking kite.'

Summer was also the time we went to Pattiamma's house in Tirunelveli. My father's parents had died before I was born, so Pattiamma, my mother's mother, was the only grandparent I knew. Appa was always too busy to accompany us. After Neela lost her husband and Maya went away to study in Chennai, only Amma and I would drive down to Pattiamma's. My mother would get very excited about these trips. The week before we left, she would go shopping to buy her mother saris and tins of imported biscuits which my grandmother loved but could not buy in her remote village. Amma was like a little girl in her enthusiasm. 'Your Pattiamma is a wonderful lady,' she would say and tell me stories about her childhood. They were very close, for Amma was Pattiamma's only surviving relative.

Pattiamma was plump and short, with permanent dimples in her cheeks. She was always happy and full of stories. Grandfather had died before my mother was born and Pattiamma had been a widow almost all her life. She lived in a huge ancient brick house, the largest in the village. I loved her house. It had a lot of secret corners. Her larder was always packed with treats, her backyard lush with fruit-laden mango trees. Her cooking was the finest I have ever tasted. I especially loved the way she served it on fresh green banana leaves. She would ask Nandi the gardener to chop the most tender leaves from the banana tree and wash them carefully. The servants would serve the food with careful ceremony. First came the pinch of salt in the left corner of the leaf. The red pickle would perch next to it, and then the golden dal and the poriyal. The meat dish, usually juicy fried chicken cooked in an earthen pot, came after this. The fluffy white rice was served in a little heap. We would dig a cosy hollow in the heap and Pattiamma would pour the spicy sambhar into it. Amma and I would eat like two little girls under her watchful gaze. I ate very cautiously so as not to tear my leafy plate.

Amma and Pattiamma spent long hours chatting under the neem tree in the backyard. This was the only time I saw my mother really relaxed. As I played I would hear their lively conversation, sprinkled with laughter, echoing through the house. It gave me a feeling of security.

I spent long lazy days looking at the numerous cows Pattiamma reared in a thatched shed at the back of her house. She loved her cows, especially the brown and white one with the swollen udder, called Rani.

Every time we visited, Pattiamma would take me on a tour of that ancient house and show me the room where my mother was born. It was a small dark room with a big bed and a huge mirror. When we visited Tirunelveli, my mother slept in that room. I slept with Pattiamma. I would cuddle up to her and inhale her special smells. Late into the night, she would tell me stories about what my mother did when she was a little girl. Amma's childhood seemed quite different from mine. 'In those days nobody bought dolls,' Pattiamma told me. 'Only the daughters of the British memsahibs had dolls. Your mother went to Bharatanatyam classes and took music lessons. She was very bright, you know, but my brothers married her off very early, because I was a widow.' I fell asleep each night soothed by the timeless drone of Pattiamma's stories.

One year I met Krishna, the untouchable boy, who came every day to milk and bathe the cows. He always wore a bangle, red stone studs in his ears and a pair of bright blue shorts that went past his knees. He never wore a shirt, only a string of multicoloured beads. He became my close friend. He was a little older than me, and very good at telling stories. Krishna would point to the huge mountain in the distance when I asked him where his house was. I found the idea of his coming every day from a distant mountain, fascinating. He told me he had once seen a huge tiger while walking down from his house to Pattiamma's. I thought that he was very brave. He became fond of me too. He would look at my dolls curiously and loved the chocolates I shared with him.

He would arrive every morning before dawn and leave at four o'clock after distributing the afternoon milk to customers. I would wake up to the sound of him sweeping and cleaning the stall where the cows stood lined up like fat military officers. In the afternoons he taught me how to fashion clay pots out of the dark brown soil he dug out from beneath the banana plants in the backyard. We made little pots and pans and stoves which we dried in the sun. He constructed a small furnace out of straw and baked the pots. He chided me when I pranced impatiently asking him to show me the pots even before they were fully baked. I loved our little games. Once he brought a parrot fledgling for me. Amma scolded him for stealing it from the parent birds. But I was charmed with the idea of having a talking bird. Before we left for home that year, I entrusted my pet into his care and begged him to keep it for me until I returned.

It was two years before we visited Pattiamma again. I was no longer a child. I waited eagerly to see Krishna and ask him about my parrot. He came at dawn. He looked slightly older. There was a faint darkening on his upper lip where his moustache had started to grow. 'Krishna!' I called. He looked up at me. But he did not come running to me like before. He did not wrinkle up his nose at my clothes as he used to, or ask for chocolates. He looked away shyly. I felt a tide of disappointment rise in me.

After Pattiamma died, I never saw Krishna again. That memorable phase of my life soon faded into a colourful memory. During the years of my marriage, when I lived through the cold winters of Darjeeling, the warm summer smells of my childhood would return to haunt me. My mind would fill with the flavours of mangoes and lime, and the chatter of the servants, and I would remember with longing those idyllic moments that would never be mine again.

FOUR

Over the next six years Maya completed her medical course. She scored the highest marks in the MBBS final exam in the state, and many newspapers carried interviews with her. Many people called to congratulate Appa, who was very pleased by all the publicity. It was then that she told him that she had secured a seat for postgraduate specialization in neurology in a very prestigious college in the US, and that they had awarded her full scholarship for her course as well. Appa had numerous arguments with Maya, and Amma feigned a heart attack. It all proved useless, for Maya was determined. Appa finally had to give in, and I think that the publicity she had received was the reason why he accepted her choice because he could have used his power to stop her if he had wanted to. So Maya went her own way. I had just turned eighteen and my mind was filled with colourful images of the US: Disneyland, Michael Jackson, skiing, and emancipated women. I was very excited that Maya was going to be a part of that.

My parents bade a disgruntled farewell to the jubilant Maya. A few months later, she sent us a lot of photographs. My mother almost fainted on seeing these. From her short hairstyle to her tight mini skirts, Maya had metamorphosed into an all-American girl. Appa was baffled and disappointed. Three months later something worse happened. My father's friend, who lived in Massachusetts, visited Maya. He called us to say that Maya had told him how her favourite food was beef burgers. This news devastated my parents for whom eating beef was blasphemous. But there was more to come. Some months later, she called my father and told him that she had something important to say. Amma feared the worst. She thought that Maya had fallen in love with an American boy. But what she had to say was not that. She said that she had always suspected that she was attracted to women, and her instincts had been proved right. She now had a girlfriend named Gail, and was very happy.

Appa was aghast. He yelled and shouted at Maya on the telephone, and ordered her to return home. But as always, she was unmoved. She said that her feelings towards them as a daughter had not changed and that she would visit them when they accepted her for what she was. Amma was too naïve to understand what was going on. I knew that Maya had really crossed the line now. She would never be accepted back by my traditional family. Appa forbade any mention of her name and ordered that her letters were to be returned unopened to her.

What I had not anticipated was that Maya's actions would have such enormous consequences for me. My father immediately started to look for a groom for me. Amma told me that it was my duty to save Appa's honour by marrying early. I was absolutely terrified and very alone. Neither of my sisters was around to talk to. All I could think of was Neela's marriage and what it had done to her. I pictured myself as a widow. My mother turned a deaf ear to my appeals. Before I could come to terms with the idea of marriage, my father had found a suitable boy. I was told that my future husband was eight years older than me, and that he was as rich as my father. Amma also told me that he was the close friend of the chief minister's son. All this information seemed to have nothing to do with me and my marriage. But I was not given the chance to say anything about the matter.

The wedding date was set for three months later, and these months were a period of frantic preparation for my family. I realized that those were the last months of life as I had known it. I had no idea what the future would be. All I knew was that I could not question what they were doing to me. I tried to pretend that I was happy. Amma bought vast amounts of stainless steel and brass vessels and many other things for my future home. I remember looking at the beautiful saris and touching the fine materials. At one level, I could not help being excited by the expensive gifts that were going to be given to me, and that they were for my new life made me look at them with a subtle sensitivity. I had always known that I would be married, and it was impossible not to get caught up in the preparations, but there was a nagging sense of discomfort. Something told me that the marriage did not augur well. I tried hard to suppress this thought. After all, my parents had chosen well for Neela and they had told me that my husband-to-be was from a good family, rich and well connected. My mother worried constantly about me and gave me a list of instructions about what to do after marriage. She knew that I had an adventurous spirit, and this she considered taboo in a good wife.

This was a period of innocence. I walked through the house looking at all the familiar things and the places that held special meaning: the little corner where I had sat and read stories to my dolls, the backyard and the sweet-smelling kitchen. I felt I had to imprint these things in my memory for I would never have them again. I would never be Aradhana, the youngest daughter of my parents. I would just be Aradhana, wife of Divakar. I tried uttering the name Divakar. The sound rang hollow in my ears, heavy yet empty. I thought of films I had seen. The celluloid heroes romanced their wives and built wonderful lives for them. Perhaps my new husband would woo me to win my love. I thought of the way in which Shivakumar had loved Neela. I wanted to experience such love. Every week some relative from Divakar's family came to visit me. I sat through these interviews with a mixture of detachment and fear. As doomsday drew close, I had an urge to run away. I had visions of me dressed in the crimson finery of a bride creeping out of the house in the dead of night.

The house was busy with preparations for weeks before the actual day of the wedding. The walls were freshly painted and the furniture gleamed with polish. Special basmati rice was ordered from the Punjab. The storeroom in the backyard was stocked with pure pulses, tins of oil and sacks of vegetables. Ten goats were tethered in the garden and fed special grains. There was a huge non-vegetarian dinner scheduled for the day before the wedding and a huge vegetarian dinner for the wedding day itself. Mubarak, the expert Mughlai cook, was hired to make the biryani.

My mother insisted on haldi and mehendi ceremonies the day before the wedding, though these were essentially north Indian rituals. Because of Neela's tragic widowhood, she wanted to ensure that I had a flawless ceremony. Appa agreed too. The haldi ceremony was conducted by an old woman with a long married life. I sat like a statue as they ceremoniously oiled my body and applied fresh turmeric, ground to a paste with a stone mortar and pestle. Then the women rubbed shikakai powder into my hair and massaged it in meticulously. They sang songs as they poured pots of water on my head to complete the ritual bath. I was then dressed in a yellow sari—yellow being considered the colour of prosperity and well-being. Then the mehendi ceremony began. A woman famed for her skill in applying mehendi on the hands and feet of brides was brought in. I sat with sleepy eyes as she painstakingly applied the green paste in delicate patterns of flowers and creepers on my palms and wrists. Young girls sang religious songs all through the night, and there was much merry banter. Amma smiled happily at me from time to time. Revathy Athai applied a huge dot of black kohl on my left cheek to ward off the evil eye. On the morning of the wedding, I was bathed again. The mehendi turned a brilliant red. 'That is a very good sign,' my aunts exclaimed, 'she will have a long and prosperous married life.'

My crimson wedding sari was of pure tissue, alternate threads of silk and gold woven together, inlaid with zari and embroidered with mangoes and elephants. Appa had had it made especially for me. When it had arrived twenty-three days before the wedding, everyone had gathered around to see it and had gasped in admiration. The blouse was made of gold tissue stitched with pearls. Dressed in this intricately spun web of silk and gold, I made a radiant bride. My hands and throat were all but encased in gold, my eyes darkened with kohl and my tumbling dark hair set in a fashionable twist with a jewel-encrusted gold tiara resting snugly on it. I recall looking at myself in the mirror and feeling a sense of pride.

The ceremony was conducted in a huge hall with a large dais decorated with flower garlands. The sacred fire burned in the middle of this dais. The fat priest was pouring ghee to keep the fire going as I walked in to take my place, accompanied by the women of my family. The rustle of the sari rose above the tinkle of my anklets and the soft murmur of the bangles that danced at my wrists, creating the beautiful music of a bride walking to her groom. At that moment I forgot my fear of marriage. It was impossible not to feel the romance of this moment of glittering confusion as I had my first glimpse of the stranger who would be my husband.

I saw two men in identical sherwanis sitting before the fire. One had a handsome face and he looked at me with acute interest. I met his deep gaze with my own. He must be the groom. But as they sat me down, I realized that it was the sober-faced one who was the groom. I riveted my gaze on him. He did not look up at me. His face was rather unattractive, and had a hint of cruelty. I did not like him and my heart lurched. He kept pouring the ghee into the fire. I looked at him through the searing flames again. He looked up at me and caught my gaze. I smiled at him. It was an intense moment. He did not smile back. There was no emotion on his face, not even a trace of warmth. His eyes cruised over my body shrouded in that jubilant material. I lowered my eyes to his fingers. I thought of those fingers touching me and I cringed inside.

The priest started chanting unfamiliar Sanskrit mantras which we were asked to repeat. I responded softly. I felt completely numb as the ceremony continued. The tali was circulated amongst the guests to be blessed. When it came back, Divakar started to put it around my neck. Then, as his hand touched my hair, I felt the tiara set on my head fall off and roll with a receding thud down the marble steps of the dais, much to the shock of the assembled guests and to my own intense embarrassment. A collective gasp echoed around the room and someone hurried to set it back on my head. I looked up at the stranger who was to be my husband. I could see that the accident had angered him. It seemed a bad omen. From the corner of my eye, I saw my mother wiping away a tear.

The rest of the ceremony went off well. The priest joined our hands together and asked us to walk around the sacred fire. When Divakar held my hand, I found no warmth there. I felt no sense of security, my heart did not beat faster; I experienced none of the surging emotions my girlfriends had said I would feel the first time my husband clasped my hand. The tali sat like a heavy weight around my neck, a cube of ice against my breast. I touched it with numb, nervous fingers.

Through the reception that followed, I sat like a doll. Divakar did not attempt to speak to me. It was weird to sit with this stranger to whom that simple ceremony had suddenly given so much power over me. I felt that I no longer belonged to me. My hands, with their many gold rings and mehendi, did not feel like a part of my body any more. The acrid smell of the dying fire and the decaying fragrance of the wilting flowers—that had been firm and beautiful when the ceremony began a few short hours ago—filled my nostrils. The banana plants anchored on either side of the pandal bent low as though in weariness. The guests left slowly, chewing betel leaves. The beating of the mridangam and the blowing of the nadaswaram stopped abruptly. There was an eerie silence in the huge hall. I glanced at him again with tired eyes. He was engrossed in low-toned discussion with his mother and seemed oblivious to me at his side.

We left quietly for my parents' house from where I would leave for my husband's home. The next time I came back, it would not be the same. My parents would treat me like a guest because now I was their married daughter. I belonged to another man and another family. The three toe-rings on each foot indicated this. The heavy yellow of the mangalsutra hanging around my neck made the same gloomy statement. If I was lucky, I thought tiredly, I might begin to love him, like Appa and Amma love each other, or Neela and Shivakumar had loved each other.

My in-laws had an ancestral home in Madurai and I was taken there the day after the wedding. It was an old house, huge, dark and constructed in traditional style. My husband was born and raised there before his parents moved to Delhi. It was there that our honeymoon night— the shanti muhurtam—would take place. This was usually three days after the wedding, but the exact time was determined by an astrologer. The day after my wedding, my mother-in-law summoned the family priest to select an auspicious day. The week after my wedding had some inauspicious days, so the shanti muhurtam was scheduled for the following Friday, seven days later. Until that day I was to sleep in my mother-in-law's room.

In the days immediately after the wedding, I barely saw Divakar. We met only at meal times when we were allowed to sit together, but we never spoke. In the evenings, we visited his relatives, accompanied by his parents. By the time Friday arrived, we had barely had a five-minute conversation with each other. That evening, I was dressed in the beautiful white silk sari with an exquisite red border customary for this ceremony. The white symbolized virginity, and the red indicated prosperity in married life. My mother-in-law had asked me to apply a lot of turmeric during my bath. The turmeric was supposed to bring marital bliss. Some woman with a very loud voice and rough hands brushed and braided my hair. Long strands of jasmine mixed with sweet-smelling champa flowers were woven into my braid. Divakar's cousin Roopa, who was considered their family beauty expert, was summoned to apply make-up on my face. I disliked her taste in clothes and the too-obvious layer of foundation on her face. Roopa bleached my face until it was stinging and then layered it with pink foundation and a generous coating of powder. She looked pleased with the effect, and my mother-in-law was elated. I was not so ecstatic because my face seemed purple to me. I preferred my natural brown complexion.

My mother-in-law took me into the puja room. She prayed to the gods that my union with Divakar would be fruitful and that we would be blessed with a son. I was led into Divakar's bedroom by a group of chattering girls. The door closed on their smothered giggles. He was not in the room. I looked around with some curiosity. It was a large room, filled with expensive pieces of furniture thrown together with no particular regard to how well they went together. There was a photograph of him peering ominously at me from the gleaming cedar dresser. Suddenly I felt very lonely and my heart longed for the security of my own home.

I sat on the bridal bed, sleep tugging at my eyelids, a cold chill enveloping my heart. I knew that my new husband would expect me to sleep with him. My knowledge of sex was limited. It was a wild jumble of words like fallopian tube and ovaries, terms my twelfth standard science teacher had recited in her thin voice. She had been a skinny woman with horn-rimmed glasses perched precariously on her ill-shaped nose, and would pronounce ovaries as 'ovariiizzz'. What my mother had merely told me was that he would touch me and that I should not object. My friend Selvi had got married six months before. She told me that her husband had not touched her until they got to know each other. I hoped that my husband would do the same.

It was a beautiful evening. There was a big yellow moon staring at me through the window, lighting up the darkened room. The room smelled of incense and flowers. Satin pillows sat on the bed like silent spectators. On the table by the bed, there was a silver pot of sweetened milk embellished with nuts and a tray of fruits. It was a romantic scene, but I felt only fear. I remembered my husband's expression of pride and boredom during the ceremony. He had not even smiled at me or said a kind word. There was a gnawing feeling in my stomach that I was doomed, and I had a desperate urge to flee. The twenty minutes that I sat there waiting for him felt like eternity.

Finally he walked in. It was the first time I was alone with a man, and a faint blush coloured my cheeks. I glanced at him; he still looked indifferent. I lowered my eyes. I poured out the glass of milk as I had been instructed and offered it to him. He took it from me and downed it in one shot. Amma had told me that he would offer me a sip of the milk, but that did not happen. I continued to look down. I heard him light a cigarette. I could see the tip glowing red in the dim light, and the acrid smell of nicotine slowly started to fill the room. He asked me if I had showered. I nodded mutely, wondering why he asked. He burped loudly. I suddenly did not want that loud obnoxious being to touch me. My heart was beating rapidly and my palms were sweating. I moved to the far corner of the bed, but even that was not enough. I wanted to disappear; for the bed to cave in and swallow me.

He lay down heavily on the bed and propped himself up on one elbow. He pushed a lock of hair from my forehead and tilted my chin. 'Are you experienced?' I looked up at him, startled. 'Hey, don't put on that frightened doe look for me. Answer me, are you a virgin?' His grip on my chin tightened. The sudden stab of pain made me wince involuntarily. My eyes began to well with tears. I tried to move out of his reach, but he was on top of me before I knew it.

'I am going to find out a few truths now,' he rasped. I closed my eyes, as if by blotting him out of my vision, I could remove him from my consciousness.

'Open your eyes. Don't I know what you rich girls do? All you do with your father's money is buy yourselves fancy clothes and gigolos. Tell me, Aradhana, how many of your male servants have you slept with?' He tugged at my sari as he spoke. It came away easily in his hands, the silk searing and cutting my skin as he pulled. 'You have a good body.'

I wished desperately that he would find me so unattractive that he would not want to touch me. By the time he undressed himself, I was truly frightened. I had never seen a man in such close proximity before, and his nakedness alarmed me. He started to caress me roughly. I was too scared to resist. My world was reduced to this beast crushing me to death. I closed my eyes, hot tears flowing down my cheeks. I stuffed my fist into my mouth to stifle a scream. I knew that any sound would only aggravate him further. I knew that I was his property and that he could do with me as he pleased. He was panting and heaving, and then he spurted something slimy on my inner thighs. I did not know what that substance was. I felt a wet dirty feeling seep into my body, but lay there silently, my eyes tightly shut. He got up, lit a cigarette and went into the washroom.

I did know that he had to penetrate me in order to consummate the marriage. I had heard aunts and cousins talking in hushed tones about the pain that accompanied a woman's first sexual intercourse. Even in my stark humiliation and misery, my brain told me that that act had not happened. I wondered if he had noticed. He seemed nonchalant. I wanted to shower immediately and wash away his touch. But I could not move.

In the faint light of the bedroom, I saw him return from the washroom. He lay down and went to sleep as if nothing had happened. It took me a while to take a grip on myself. By the time I gathered the courage to go into the shower, he was snoring loudly and the pearly light of dawn was creeping in through the slender slats of the window blinds. I stood in the scorching water trying to erase the memory of his touch on my body. The soap slithered out of my hand and the scrubbing mitt was in shreds, but I still felt unclean. It was as though he had permanently scarred me. His touch seemed to linger on upon my skin. I kept repeating the names of the numerous gods mechanically, but that did not seem to help. I spent the night crouched on the floor beside the bed, too shocked even to cry.

I was embarrassed to look at him in the morning. I could not forget that he had seen and touched my naked body. He did not even look at me until we were drinking coffee later in the morning when he turned to me with that arrogant look I had already come to despise. 'You know what, Aradhana, you are not even a good whore. I could sue your father for passing off something so inadequate to me.'

I could not understand what he was saying. I was incapable of any kind of comprehension at that moment. I knew I had not satisfied him in bed and that made me strangely happy. But this could not take away the horror of what had happened. For several nights after that, I would wake up in fear, feeling that eerie slimy liquid crawl down my thighs, and rush to the bathroom to try to wash away that imaginary grime from my body.

The very next afternoon, Divakar said that we had to leave for Darjeeling. I dreaded going to live with him in an alien pláce so far away from home. When I went to see my mother before leaving, she gave me many diverse instructions on how to be a good wife. I bade farewell to my family and quietly followed him to wherever he was taking me. I think from the very first days of my married life, I started to hate him and my heart began to fill with pain at the thought of being married to him for life.

FIVE

Awarded a new name and assigned a new role, I walked into his beautiful house in the cold and remote city of Darjeeling snuggled in the extended bosom of the Himalayas. I still remember my first glimpse of that white house with its huge granite pillars, which looked faintly pink in the evening light, set in a beautiful garden with manicured lawns. There were no relatives or friends to welcome us. The many servants stared at me with the curiosity new brides always arouse. I smiled as warmly as I could. Ratna, the housekeeper, brought out the aarati, circled it around me and Divakar, and placed a dot of red sindoor on my forehead. Someone else broke a coconut to ward off the evil eye.

Divakar asked Ratna to give me a tour of the house and disappeared into his office. I followed Ratna around silently. There had been no expense spared in decorating the house, but it was done with no taste. Our bedroom looked monstrously large, dominated by the huge bed in the centre. I looked at it with distaste, thinking of the countless nights I would have to spend in it with Divakar.

My head swam with tiredness after the long journey. Nothing seemed clear to me. I needed desperately to calm the unease rising rapidly inside me. The bathtub looked inviting. I ran a hot bath and put in some bath salts. I peeled off my clothing and slithered into the soothing warmth. As the water embraced my body, I closed my eyes and let the sense of peace seep into me.

'Hey, if you need sex, ask me. Only lusty bitches soak in tubs; decent women take showers. Get out, you whore!' I opened my eyes in shock and found myself staring into Divakar's contorted face. He pulled me out of the tub, carried me to the bedroom and dropped me on the bed in a wet quivering heap. The smell of his unwashed body as he took off his trousers and lunged at me made my stomach turn. He tore at my long hair and muttered obscenities. For all his brutality, he still could not penetrate me, and subsided after soiling my thighs. My body seemed to have a will of its own and would not let him consummate the marriage. But this time, he was furious and started to beat me. My sense of shock and horror was so intense that I could not even cry.

After he was gone, I dragged my sore body to the washroom. I knew then that I would never ever take comfort in a bath again. I unplugged the tub and listened to the gurgle of the water. I was frightened even of that mundane drone. I felt nausea rise in me and I vomited into the washbasin. It was the first of the many times I would throw up there. I took a scalding hot shower.

Slowly I forgot my dreams as I tried to mould myself to fit into the role they had cast me in. My first few months in Darjeeling were absolutely horrifying. I wondered why they had held such a lavish wedding if I had to live like a slave after it. Before the mehendi faded from my skin, my husband created brilliant red welts on my body. I wondered why the numerous gods my parents prayed to could not have protected their daughter from falling into the hands of such a cruel man.

The rooms in his house exuded coldness. I felt like an intruder as I had nothing to do with the running of the household. My husband instructed me not to mingle with the servants. I had little to do in the kitchen, the focus of my mother's household activities. It did not feel like a home, let alone my home. A stern-faced cook systematically dished out tasty food at stipulated times. My days and evenings were equally lonely. Divakar was rarely at home. He would come back at dinnertime and gobble his food without a word. He never asked me how my day had been and I never volunteered any information. At exactly ten o'clock, he would say, 'Let's sleep,' and walk to the bedroom. I would follow him quietly. In the bedroom he would ask me curt questions, which I would answer nervously. He slapped me if I said too much or too little. I slowly learned to give him the answers that he wanted, and I am sure he was happy that he was shaping me to be a proper obedient wife. If he chose to have sex, I lay down mutely and let him quell his desire. There were never any caresses or words of endearment, but he frequently hit me during sex. I often cried silently when he touched my body. Even though he knew that, he never asked why. I fell asleep each night in that sordid silence.

Darjeeling was a beautiful place with lots of open spaces. The bungalow was surrounded by a vast expanse of garden. There were huge rows of roses and long stretches of emerald green lawns. In the evenings, the smell of champa and jasmine filled the garden. I must admit I did have a charming prison.

The only person I talked to in those first few months was the gardener Ramdin. I would see him hard at work from my bedroom window as he steadily trimmed the hedges, pulled out weeds and tended the roses. Every day he brought fresh flowers into the house and arranged them in the huge bronze vases. Sometimes I would chat with him in the morning. He loved it when I admired his handiwork. He reminded me of Krishna. Krishna must have been around Ramdin's age. I wondered where he was, and whether he was married and had children.

Ramdin told me the histories of different trees, the fruit of his many years' work in the garden. 'I have lived in this bungalow for ten years—since I was thirteen. This garden is my temple. Before Divakar sahib bought this house five years ago, Mrs Simmons owned it. She was some lady. She had pure British blood in her. Her husband died in India during British rule. That was why she wanted to die here too. She was not only my mistress, she was a good friend too. It is because of her that I speak good English.' He cleared his throat proudly.

I was fascinated by the story of Mrs Simmons. I imagined a charming old lady living in this house in memory of a very loving husband. Ramdin started to talk again as if he had read my thoughts. 'This house was full of fun then. Mrs Simmons had a lot of friends. She was such a happy soul. Every afternoon at four o'clock she would make me a cup of tea and serve it in wafer-thin china cups painted with roses. I was very sad when she died. It was as if I had lost a mother. Then Divakar sahib bought this house.' He stopped, but I felt that he did not like his new employer. I asked him why he continued working here. 'I love this garden,' he told me. 'Mrs Simmons and I planted most of these trees together. I will not let any other person meddle with her garden. When she was dying, I promised her that I would take care of her garden.' I liked Ramdin. He was the one person in the house who seemed to have a heart.

When Divakar was not around, I gradually started chatting with the servants, though he had forbidden me to. I dreamed a lot, especially of running away. I imagined tearing away my finery and jewels, letting my abundant hair free and running wild in the fields. I thirsted for freedom. I had grown up knowing that I would one day be some man's wife, but somehow, I could not fit into conventional married life. I performed all my duties, but my heart wasn't in anything I did. It was always wandering through the mountains and flitting amidst the butterflies.

When Divakar was home, I retreated into my shell and became quiet, obedient and duty-conscious. I hated Sundays because he stayed home. I had to pour him fourteen cups of tea—not one more, not one less—at regular intervals. The cook would prepare the tea and pour it into a huge blue flask. At a nod from Divakar, I would have to pour out tea for him while he sat watching satellite television or staring at the computer. The cook usually made chicken biryani and lamb curry on Sundays. Divakar would eat and then leave for his game of golf at exactly three o'clock. He came back at seven, smelling of cigarettes and turf and sweat. My nostrils would rebel against that Sunday smell. At 7:15 he would have sex with me. On Sundays, it was worse than on other days. He was rougher and more obscene. At 7:30 it would be over. I would drag myself to the shower, while he slept in his own filth.

Slowly I adapted myself to the ways of that house and its master, though there was always a sense of shock that this was the way my life was turning out to be. I felt cheated out of my youth and happiness. My mother had told me that marriage demanded obedience, but not that it meant accepting constant insult and abuse. Obedience, I had displayed, but to no effect. I wondered dully whether if I had known that marriage was like this, I would have somehow had enough strength to escape it.

In the early days, when I was still actively rebelling against this life that I was forced to lead, I wrote a letter to my mother telling her about my strange and sorry life. I wanted to know why it was that I had to live like this. I was beautiful and silent, like the dolls that I used to play with. I asked my mother if this was all that my life would hold. My restless mind could not adapt the way my body had.

Amma never answered that letter. She probably found it too shocking and brutal. I knew that often it was reporting abuse that was considered the crime, not the abuse itself. Maybe she tore my letter to shreds so that Appa would never find it. Amma's silence haunted me.

I wanted her so desperately to respond to my need, to tell me that I had done no wrong. But she was silent. Every day when the khaki-uniformed mailman arrived at the door, I rushed to scan the pile of letters for my mother's rounded handwriting. My eyes would sting with tears when disappointment greeted me yet again. I became almost angry with Amma. It was as if I had knocked at her door and she had refused to let me in. I had believed that she was my friend, and now she had betrayed me. Now I realize that I did not understand the reason for her terrible silence. It was an expression of her own lack of freedom.

But my greatest sense of shock came some months later when we visited my parents for some religious ceremony. I had been looking forward to this for weeks. When we reached Madurai, my house was already swarming with relatives. There were garlands of golden marigolds adorning the walls and the house was full of tantalizing smells of delicious food. The priest sat in the centre of the hall, pouring yellow ghee into the sacred fire. I peeped into the backyard where the feast was being prepared amidst much noise and confusion. Little boys sat peeling piles of pink onions and chopping spicy green chillies into jade heaps. There were numerous cauldrons sitting on stone stoves, frothing with milk-white rice and sambhar, supervised by cooks sweating profusely in the heat. A particularly obese cook was busy dipping boondhi into ghee and making laddoos. Gopal, our family cook, greeted me fondly and invited me to have a first taste of the food. I walked back into the house, my nose tingling with the aromas.

In the crowded hall, everyone was looking at me because I was newly married, and my expensive clothes and fine jewellery indicated to them that all was well. My aunt Meenakshi, whose daughter had recently married a primary school teacher, was especially impressed with my heavy gold chain and matching bangles, and kept repeating how fortunate I was to have been born rich and married rich. Divakar walked around with Appa, who was proudly introducing his prosperous son-in-law to his guests.

I spotted two of my former classmates in the crowd. I went over to them and soon we were chatting happily about our silly girlhood games and old friends. They were married too, but none of us talked about the present. It was just good to remember old and innocent times.

Divakar must have stood behind me for quite a while. I didn't hear him call me until one of my friends pointed it out. I stood up and turned to face him. I could see that he was angry, and I hurriedly started apologizing for not hearing him. Before I could finish, he gave me a stinging slap, right in front of the assembled guests. Tears filled my eyes and through that salty screen, I saw my parents stand like silent spectators. For an instant I was sure that my father would come to my rescue. But that fantasy was short-lived. Divakar grabbed my hand and dragged me to the guest bedroom. As we left the hall, I could see my father turn to one of the guests and resume his conversation as if nothing had happened. Once we were in the room and the door was firmly shut, Divakar grabbed me by the hair and started to beat me mercilessly. Over his curses, I could hear the sounds of laughter and chatter outside. There was a strange sense of unreality that my immediate family and friends were in fact a few feet away, tucking into the sumptuous meal and talking gaily, while Divakar was beating me. He left me there in tears and went out to join the party.

I cried till my eyes were dry. I felt so miserable that I was in my father's home where I should feel protected and safe, but nobody loved me enough to speak up for me. This sense of being unwanted settled into me with a heavy silence and left me feeling very alone. I looked out of the window and saw the lush green branches of the guava tree in the garden. The garden where I had happily built mud houses, planted little gardens of my own and cooked make-believe food in its shade when I was a child. I could have never imagined that the house I would have in real life would be filled with blood and tears. As the day melted into evening, the guests left, and the house grew quiet. I heard my father offering Divakar a drink. I kept expecting my parents to come and try to comfort me. But nobody did.

The only thing my father ever said about this whole episode was that I should have been more attentive to Divakar rather than engaging in idle chatter with my friends. My mother pretended nothing had happened. I had never felt more let down before. Before this, when Divakar would beat me in Darjeeling, I would console myself that when I told my parents all about my suffering, they would take me away from him. During the long journey back to Darjeeling, I realized that I did not even have this option to fall back on.

This was reinforced when my parents came to visit us

for our first anniversary. The gifts that the bride's parents are to give on this occasion are customarily decided before the wedding. My mother-in-law and father-in-law had arrived the day before my parents' arrival, as if to check whether they had fulfilled the agreement. My parents had brought clothes for me and Divakar, jewellery and other gifts— much more than what they had promised to give. They had even bought a red-and-gold brocade sari for my mother-in-law. She weighed it in her plump, greedy palms and smiled smugly. There was a Rolex watch for my father-in-law.

Everything went well until lunchtime, when my mother-in-law suddenly saw my long fingernails and said, 'Oh, Divakar allows you to grow your nails.' I did not think that Divakar had ever noticed my fingernails before this.

But now he came over to me, grabbed my hands and peered at my fingernails. 'How long have you had these?'

I did not answer him but withdrew my palms hastily.

He walked away and I hoped that that was the end of the issue. But he came back with a pair of nail clippers and roughly took my fingers in his own. He started to cut them very close until my fingertips were bleeding. The drops of blood slowly seeped into my pale blue sari. I tried hard to stifle my sobs. All around us, our parents sat in silence as if nothing was happening. My mother was seriously studying the lotus pattern on her sari, my mother-in-law continued slurping her badaam kheer. When he was done with all ten fingers, I covered my bloody fingertips in the folds of my sari and retreated into the relative comfort of my room.

And so my strange life continued, except that now the last hope of escape or protest had disappeared. In the freezing winds and biting chill of Darjeeling, I sat in my cold and eerie home, trying to remember what warmth felt like. Darjeeling is a beautiful town but the beauty around me was rendered desolate by the emptiness in my life. I often contemplated escaping from that house of horror, but I doubted whether my parents would ever take me back.

I thought of Madurai and my home with intense longing. I remembered the special smells and sounds of my mother's house, where though there were many rules, there was still warmth. I could picture the huge pickle jar in the corner of the pantry and hear the cacophony of the crows as they tried to steal the grains spread to dry on the terrace; the gentle sound of my mother's feet on the mosaic floor, and the dhobi beating heavy blankets against the ancient washing stone in the backyard. Lying in my cold marital bed, I craved for the scent of the eucalyptus oil that my mother always put in the last rinse when washing the sheets. The noises in Darjeeling seemed frightening and alien, even the birdsong sounded strange. There was no music in life any more, only the stark clatter of empty routine.

For most of the week, I read novels, watched soaps on television or gazed at Ramdin work in garden. The only variations in the routine were Thursdays and Saturdays. Thursday was the cook's day off and I would do the cooking. I longed for Thursdays because there was something to do with my day. I would take my time chopping onions, tending to the simmering curry and stirring the chattering vegetables in the frying pan. I would cook for all the servants, so they would not bring along their lunch in their little aluminium lunch boxes on that day. It was a pleasure to watch them eat heartily. Divakar did not object to these little lunch parties; perhaps he did not notice them for he rarely concerned himself with what went on in the house. He ate my food with indifference.

On Saturdays Divakar entertained at home. He would order fluffy parathas and red chicken curry from an exclusive Mughlai restaurant. These parties were very boring for me. The guests were a combination of big or small politicians whom Divakar befriended as insurance against times of emergency, business colleagues and hangers-on to whom Divakar could play the benevolent host. My role was to be well dressed and silent. I played that role well. It was easy to be quiet. None of the men brought their wives along. I had to stay up until the last guest left. And then Divakar would make some caustic comment on something I had said or done. I never answered him, but went to bed silently.

I enjoyed Saturday mornings, though. I would go to the market with Ratna to supervise the weekly grocery shopping. The market in Darjeeling was noisy but fun. I liked visiting the little wooden vegetable shacks where the vendors sat with wicker baskets full of their magnificent fare: plump scarlet tomatoes, onions packed with promises of tears, pearl-white garlic hiding their pungent odours, dainty hillocks of lady's fingers, green and red chillies, and a variety of gourds. At the fruit stalls, bunches of golden bananas, tiny sweet Simla apples and shiny purple and green grapes drove the flies into a frenzy. The meat shops displayed freshly slaughtered and skinned goats with their tails still attached to their exposed hips. Bleating goats and frenzied chickens in crowded coops awaited the butcher's axe. Tribal hunters hawked wild quails, partridges and other identifiable and unidentifiable birds with promises of renewed virility, long life and even prosperity. Amidst this pandemonium squatted rows of chattering women weaving strands of flowers for sale. From the famous Darjeeling teashops with their huge bronze and copper boilers wafted exotic fragrances. This was one of my few contacts with life outside the house and I enjoyed it immensely.

Another source of enjoyment was taking long walks in the sprawling estate that surrounded the house. Darjeeling will always remain one of the most beautiful places I have seen, and the fragrance springing from the tea bushes was intoxicating. But as I paced slowly amidst these exquisite gardens, I would inevitably begin to feel melancholic that I had no one to enjoy this glorious experience with. It was not so much when I was unhappy but when I was happy, that my sense of intense loneliness became most acute. When I heard a beautiful song on the radio, or when the sun peeped out in wintry weather and sneaked through the windows into the house, I would flush with pleasure and quickly pale as I realized that I had no one whose enjoyment of the same experience would enhance my joy. Boring days had at least this virtue that they did not inspire pain or acute desolation in me.

I sometimes wondered why Divakar had married at

all if he had no desire to share his life with his wife apart from abusing her and sleeping with her. But slowly I comprehended that he had not desired companionship when he married me; my presence simply complemented and completed the picture of domestic perfection. I fitted into the perfectly maintained façade of his life: the beautiful wife who went with the Valentino suits, the handcrafted furniture and the gorgeous house which had to be immaculate at all times. I often wondered how he could be so set in his ways at twenty-seven. He had to have the perfectly-made bed, the exquisitely-set table and the elegant living room. His tastes and hobbies befitted the gentleman he was trying to project himself as. For example, he had a fetish for collecting odd and expensive things, and he would spend hours buying, arranging and admiring his collections of pens and key chains in the so-called library where no books were ever read.

One of my regular duties as his wife was to maintain cordial relations with his parents and siblings, who all lived in Delhi. I had to call them regularly at 11 a.m., and receive my mother-in-law's instructions about how to take care of Divakar. Initially, I did not find this very difficult, but I sometimes wondered why my mother-in-law could not be more understanding or affectionate. If I was too friendly, she complained that I was not respectful enough. If I was too polite, I was called high and mighty. Gradually, I became more anxious about this ritual and I would practise nervously before dialling her number.

One day in early autumn, about two years after my marriage, my restlessness and hopelessness became intolerable. As I sat in front of the huge glass window, I saw the red-gold leaves drifting down from the trees and the bright colours of the late chrysanthemums throbbing within the garden. It was cold and the sky was overcast. Sparrows pecked at blades of grass. Other birds sang out to one another as the time of evening rest drew near. Nature looked so abundant as it prepared to settle into slumber. I huddled into my cashmere shawl, my heart heavy with sadness, my young body trembling with sorrow because it was familiar only with pain. I wondered why Divakar hated me so much. I knew I was beautiful, but why was it that my beauty inspired no love in him? Why did he want to squeeze out every drop of youth and joy that ran in my veins? Why was it that he so obviously desired me, yet only wanted to inflict pain? I had grown up reading romantic novels that spoke of the comforting strength of a loving man's arms wrapped around you, and of the quiet companionship which love created. I longed for the fulfilment of love; to bring purpose into my still life and open up my cloistered spirit.

At that point, I decided quite suddenly that I would run away. If I went back home, my parents would surely not refuse to keep me with them if I was desperate. I knew it was considered dishonourable for the family if a married daughter left her husband's house and came back to the parental home. But my parents loved me. The thought of home gave me sudden resolution and courage.

I took a wad of notes from the locker and left the house. From the small station in Darjeeling, I took a train to Calcutta. In Calcutta, I squeezed myself into a lowly second-class compartment of the Coromondal Express that would take me to Chennai. The two nights on the train passed like a dream. I had never travelled on my own before, nor had I ever travelled second class. I sat in my filthy seat while harried and sweaty passengers dragged screaming children and stuffed them into the overcrowded compartment, not quite believing that I was actually doing this.

I finally managed to complete the series of train and bus journeys and reached home three days after I had set out. It was about two in the afternoon. I felt a surge of fear as I got off the auto-rickshaw and stood in front of the gate. I nodded to the gatekeeper as he opened it, an expression of surprise in his eyes. I rang the doorbell, and one of the maids let me in. Amma was in the living room, sitting in her favourite chair, sewing. I went and stood in front of her, but I did not dare to meet her eye. She looked up and almost screamed. The three days in the train and bus had left my face and clothes streaked with dirt, and my hair dry and covered with dust.

'Where have you been?'

'I left him,' I said and sank into the sofa.

'Aradhana, I cannot believe you did this. We heard from Divakar that you were missing. Appa is really upset. You should go back to your husband.'

I closed my eyes. My fatigue was too much. My mother's words did nothing to ease the tension. She sat beside me. I thought that I saw a hint of concern in her eyes.

'Aradhana, you should shower. Appa must not see you like this.' She stroked my hair.

I had a long hot shower in the familiar bathroom. It was wonderful. I watched the rivulets of water run down my body and gather in puddles around my feet. It felt nice to use the Mysore sandal soap that Amma always kept in our washrooms. That smell belonged to my childhood and to idyllic summer days. I dressed in a cool green sari printed with purple flowers, and went downstairs. Amma had a hot meal ready for me. I tucked into the fluffy rice and vegetables without a word. She said nothing as she spooned the food out onto my plate. The familiar flavours tasted like manna.

As I was eating, my father arrived. The sound of his footstep in the hallway squashed my appetite. I looked at my mother. She avoided my eyes and went to meet him. Amma took Appa into their bedroom as she always did when they had something important to discuss. I washed my hands and retreated upstairs. I was too frightened to see my father. I felt a tightness clutch my throat and travel through my body. I knew that he would ask me to return to Darjeeling.

Amma came upstairs after a while. 'Aradhana,' she said, 'Appa is very upset that you left your husband's home. You should not have done that. Anyway, he will phone Divakar today and try to get him to take you back.'

I was shocked. Somehow I could not believe that after all this, Appa wanted to send me back to Divakar right away. A sense of cold horror ran through me. I looked at Amma. 'Amma, I don't want to go there.' Tears welled up and ran slowly down my cheeks. If I went back, Divakar would treat me with even more disdain and anger.

'Aradhana, don't worry. Appa will try to convince

Divakar to forgive you.' She stroked my hair. I looked numbly out of the window. The weather was beautiful. The marigolds were in full bloom and looked like a patch of liquid gold against the emerald lawn. Their strong fragrance wafted up and tickled my nose. I turned away and looked at my mother. She looked tired but unruffled. I wondered if she really wanted to turn me away. But I could not read her expression. It was the same calm countenance she had worn during Shivakumar's funeral. Amma never displayed her feelings.

Appa spoke to Divakar that evening. Listening intently from upstairs, I could hear him apologize profusely as if I had committed a crime. I cringed inwardly. My father, who rarely if ever apologized to anybody, was speaking in such a submissive manner. From hearing my father's side of the conversation, I could make out that Divakar was being as hard on him as he could be. The conversation was brief. Amma anxiously stood next to him, waiting for him to tell her the news.

After Appa hung up, he paced up and down nervously. The only other time I could remember him doing that was at Shivakumar's funeral. He spoke to Amma in hushed tones I could not hear. I could not bear the tension that seemed to pound within my head.

Amma came upstairs to report after a few minutes. 'Divakar is very upset with the things that you have done. He wants us to call his parents and negotiate matters with them. He says that only if they agree will he take you back.'

I looked away, bitter tears smarting my eyes. I realized that I had hoped that my running away would antagonize

Divakar so much that he would not want me back. But no, my parents were summarily sending me back and Divakar was ironically belying my hopes yet again by not refusing outright to take me back.

'Don't worry, Aradhana. Appa will take care of things.' I turned to my mother and stared into her eyes. Didn't my mother want to know why I had taken the huge step of running away? Didn't she want to know what I wanted? All I saw was that serene expression again. I wished that she would open up and speak to me. Then I would be able to tell her all about my life, my loneliness, how violated I felt in his bed, and how my days were filled with an unchanging numbness. I believed firmly that she would sympathize and want to help me if she knew the truth. But she did not want to know.

Appa spoke to Divakar's parents in Delhi. They said that this was a bad time for negotiations as it was Puratasi, the month when no negotiations or auspicious things should be done. I spent that month quietly at my parents' house. It was as if I had crept back into childhood. I tried to blank out the fact that I was married and my life had changed, and enjoyed all the old things I had done before. Amma seemed happy to have me home too. In the evenings, we would sit and chat together. We both avoided any mention of Divakar or my marriage. She made me all my favourite snacks, like modaks and little puffed rice balls stuffed with nuts and jaggery. I ate them, feeling the silent comfort I knew she wanted to convey. It felt wonderful to sleep on a bed that Divakar could not invade and to wake up knowing that I would not have to look at his face. I spent hours watching

Meenatchi, the new maid, pound rice in the ancient grinding stone. She sang the most beautiful songs while she deftly landed the four-foot-tall pestle into the hollow in the middle of the grinding stone. The magic of her tunes was lulling, and strangely unreal.

It was the end of the monsoons. Every evening at five, the rains descended. I sat at the window, listening to the slow drizzle and savouring the smell of the earth soaking in the water. The mud grew saturated and ran in coffee-coloured rivulets. The newly-washed leaves and flowers shone like jewels in the fading light. I realized again how much I loved the monsoon. When the rain finally stopped late at night, I lay in my comforting bed, listening to the gentle rhythm of the errant droplets falling from the leaves, and the crickets burst into song. I had gone to sleep listening to these sounds for eighteen monsoons of my life. These were not the unfamiliar trills of Darjeeling. When I woke up every morning filled with the satisfaction of being secure, I looked out of the window again to see the garden gleaming in the light of dawn, each droplet on the leaves a prism of colour. It was so peaceful, so quiet, yet filled with such joy.

But the month was over all too soon. Divakar's father called and told my father that they were coming to Madurai to start negotiations for my return. Appa was happy and Amma tried to look happy too. I waited with dread as the day of their arrival came. It was a Friday. Amma asked me to wear a red silk sari and a garland of jasmine in my hair. I obeyed her with as much grace as I could muster. She told me to stay in my room until I was called down. I sat waiting, feeling like an escaped convict who had been caught and would soon be sent back to prison.

They came right on time. I could hear the conversation from where I was. My mother-in-law's voice boomed above the rest. Incongruously, the smells of delicious cooking wafted up from the kitchen along with the sound of angry voices. Amma was, as usual, preparing a banquet. I had seen three plump fowls waiting to be slaughtered in the backyard that morning. I felt a certain bond with them.

My mother-in-law's voice could be heard upstairs with great clarity. 'Aradhana has shamed our family. It is only after a lot of consideration that we have decided to take her back. But for that to happen, there are some things you have to do.'

'Oh, we will do anything you want,' Appa said.

After three gruelling hours of discussion, they came to a strange agreement that seemed designed to crush my pride and humiliate my family. I had to fall at the feet of my in-laws and beg for their forgiveness. Then I had to visit five temples they named, to atone for my 'sin'. My father had to sign away three acres of fertile land and give my in-laws a sum of two lakh rupees as compensation. Appa agreed to all this. I was summoned downstairs and told what I had to do. My sense of mortification as I ritually touched their feet cannot be described. My mother-in-law looked triumphant.

Bizarrely enough, we all sat down to lunch after that. I was silent and could not eat a bite. 'Eat,' my mother-in-law said. 'It is really insulting to others if you don't eat. Moreover, it shows how stubborn you still are.' Amma looked at me pleadingly. I stuffed the food into my mouth and tried to force it down my throat. After they finally left, I went upstairs and threw up until I was faint. My escape was over and I was back on death row.

After the five-temple visit my mother-in-law had decreed, Amma started to pack my bags. She purchased a lot of silk saris for me, and suits for Divakar. I stopped being frightened and passively did whatever I was asked to do. My parents accompanied me to Darjeeling, Amma reciting a series of prayers throughout the journey. I tried hard to not think about how furious Divakar would be with me. But every now and then, that thought would come back to me.

My parents went back home the afternoon after we reached. Divakar avoided looking directly at me or talking to me while they were there. As their car drove away, he finally turned and looked at me with intense scorn in his eyes. Then, he walked away. I shrank against the wall wishing the earth would open up and swallow me. The servants were still in the house, doing their routine chores. Life seemed superficially back to normal. The tension was incredible. It was like the calm of the ocean before a storm of monumental fury. I hid in my room. The hours crawled by ominously.

The servants finally left around seven. The eerie silence chilled my soul. I arranged and rearranged the perfume bottles on my dresser. I heard him enter the room. He kicked the door shut behind him. He did not say anything. I did not say anything either. There was nothing to be said. He started to hit me and when he finally stopped, the sun had already taken over reign of the heavens from the moon.

Slowly I realized that there could be no escape for me except in the cold embrace of death. The more I thought of it, the more convinced I became that I should kill myself. I started thinking obsessively about ways and means. I was scared to try to hang myself. It seemed too complicated. I wished there was an easier way to die. Finally, I thought of the little black cabinet where Divakar stored his medicines. An overdose of sleeping pills seemed easy and final.

I wrote a farewell note to my mother:

Dear Amma,
This is the last letter you will receive from me. When you receive this, I will be dead and gone. You might even refuse to read this because I escaped from the marriage you locked me into. I am sorry to cause you grief, Amma, but I cannot tolerate this any more. I am too weak to live in such a violent relationship.

Please don't think too badly of me, and try to understand what I am trying to tell you. I want you to know that I had special dreams. I wanted to be happy. I wanted to be loved. It is sad that I was denied all these simple pleasures. I have cried every single night of my marriage. I live in absolute fear of being beaten and molested by my husband. I am so frightened to live in this house. I have nowhere to go. I know now that I cannot come to your house or get comfort from you. I do not blame you, you are as much a victim as I am. I just wanted to be happy and you stopped me.

Your daughter,
Aradhana

I took out the bottle of Calmpose, and swallowed them one by one. I lay down and felt a spurt of dizziness and then a heavy drowsiness. My mind started to wander, images flitting in and out. The Tamil new year, Pongal, was just a week away. I half-dreamt of the beautiful kolams Amma and I would make with multicoloured powders for the occasion. When I was little, one Pongal morning, I had crawled into bed beside my sleeping father, wanting to wish him as soon as he woke up. I lay down quietly, inhaling his special smells and listening to his steady breathing. I put one small hand on his arm. Suddenly, he was awake. For a split second I thought that he was going to hug me. But he looked embarrassed and admonished me for crawling into his bed. Shamefacedly I trudged back to my own bed. I cried for Appa's caresses in my drowsy state. Then there was darkness.

I woke up many hours later in a strange bed with a sense of wonder and disappointment that I was still alive. I tried to lift my arm and winced in pain. Through hazy eyes I saw Divakar staring at me. He had an expression of triumph painted on his face. I shut my eyes immediately. They had saved me. Silent tears slid through my closed eyelids. I did not even have the freedom to die. I was doomed. I have never felt so absolutely alone and desolate in my life.

The years passed and I became more and more silent. I stopped looking for escape. The private world in my mind was like the ocean, constantly heaving and whispering mysterious messages. But outwardly I was as still as a sheet of glass, like a silent shadow. I conformed as silently and passively as possible to all of Divakar's demands. Resisting violence had only given pain. Staying still and quiet became a matter of survival, and sheltered me from most of his wrath. My life and body were both barren. Our unfulfilling and incomplete sexual relations could not make me a mother. It was impossible that a life could be created where there was so much hatred and horror. I was devoid of emotion. I stopped enjoying music, and neither beautiful flowers nor the lingering magic of the rain aroused any response in me.

Divakar held me responsible for my barrenness. He told me I was deformed and doomed to die a virgin. My humiliation and sense of abject failure were so great that I accepted his verdict that I was totally inadequate as a woman in the real sense of the word. I knew I felt nothing when he touched me and I would lie with clenched teeth and closed fists, waiting for him to ejaculate and get off me. I did not have any pride left in me. The core of me was vacant like an abandoned well; even my eyes lost all expression. Yet somewhere deep inside my heart, there was a sense of satisfaction that my marriage was not consummated. However much he battered my body externally, he still could not reach the core as he could not touch the integrity of my soul. As five long years passed, this was the one thought that kept me at least partly alive. I felt strangely insulated against my predator.

S I X

I knew I looked beautiful that evening. The midnight blue sari descended in soft waves around my ankles like a sliver of the night sky that had fallen upon the earth. I surveyed the room. Ratna had arranged it to perfection. The table was set with crisp lace, and sparkling silver and crystal. Tall scented candles glowed in the corners, creating pools of warmth. I slowly arranged the blue flowers on the marble mantelpiece, coaxing in sprigs of baby's breath amidst the vibrant blooms. The house gleamed, resplendent in its splendour. Divakar entertained a lot. His profession demanded that of him. He was a good host and I had learnt to play the perfect hostess. People loved the parties that he threw, and commented on what a good couple we made.

I stared at myself in the huge mirror over the mantelpiece. My image looked back at me. I looked serene and composed—a vision of perfect harmony. The world considered me a fortunate woman. I had a gorgeous home, and a husband who made a lot of money. Only I knew the hollowness within. The tears started to gather slowly, but I checked myself. Divakar would be home any moment with the guests, and I had to look happy.

The doorbell pierced the silence. I quickly donned my social smile and waited for the servant to usher the guests in. The evening drifted on with its familiar monotony. Divakar's parties were always a lavish success. Entertaining his friends had become quite easy for me. Many years of doing this helped me to perform mechanically, though there was never anyone interesting to talk to. They all seemed charming on the surface. But then, so was Divakar. All men were the same. On this desolate thought, I looked up and found myself staring into a pair of very interested brown eyes.

'Mark Stratton,' he said, and extended his hand towards me.

I put my slender brown fingers in his strong hand and whispered, 'Aradhana. Aradhana Divakar.' A smile lit up his eyes as though he was having a private joke and I hastily withdrew my hand.

'Nice to meet you,' he said softly.

I don't know what was happening to me but I felt an instant bond with him. We talked—I don't remember what about—but he laughed easily and made me laugh too. It had been a long time since I had laughed freely. I found the way he concluded his sentences with the typically Canadian 'eh', very endearing.

Mark was twenty-nine, a software consultant from Canada who knew Divakar through professional connections. Divakar wanted Mark to work for him on his international software ventures. This was why he was extra cordial to him, and he had warned me to make a special effort to talk to him. I was ready to say my usual, polite 'hello', I had just not expected to meet someone whom I could talk to.

Mark entered my life with a silent surety. I cannot even begin to describe the heady thrill of talking to him the first few times that we met. When I think of the way in which I fell in love with him, it seems almost unbelievable. I wonder now how in my numb and frightened state I had managed to reach out and find love in another man. The human mind is a strangely resilient thing. My spirit, repressed these five long years, fought valiantly to preserve my childhood assumption that life was beautiful.

At dinner at our house one night soon after this— Divakar was following up his plan of wooing Mark conscientiously—I was seated next to Mark. I felt I glowed with a noticeable radiance when I was with him. I took a sip of my drink nervously and then redid my lipstick. 'Aradhana, you don't have to do that to look good. You look even more lovely with your lipstick smudged,' he whispered into my ear, his eyes glinting mischievously. I was startled but happy that he was looking at me so closely.

Mark visited Divakar often and I looked forward to these visits. While he talked business with Divakar, I sat in the living room, pretending to leaf through a pile of glossy magazines but actually concentrating on catching every word or glimpse that I could manage. All these years, I had wanted a friend to talk to without realizing how badly I wanted it. I felt miserable when the servants left the house in the evening. And a great part of my joy now was at having a friend with whom I could talk and laugh.

I always felt shy when I was with him, though my mind and heart turned unusually vocal. He would sometimes ask me if I was uncomfortable, as if he had sensed my reserve. He tried his best to joke with me and put me at ease. It seemed strange that though I had known him for such a short time, I enjoyed his company so much that when I was with him, I would anticipate his eventual departure with the grief befitting the departure of an old friend. I missed him even while he was with me, regretting the passing of the hour of ease.

After I met Mark, I landed right back in the world of the living. I realized with great joy and a sense of amazement that my spirit was not dead after all, but had only been in hibernation. Just as a rare orchid blooms with the right balance of light, moisture and warmth, I blossomed in the environment that Mark created when he was with me. My days that had seemed to stretch before me like a never-ending desert, now began to assume life and colour. Whenever Mark was included in Divakar's parties, I dressed with extra care. I savoured his every gesture and word. The mention of his name was enough to thrill me. It was as if a secret spring had sprung within me and was rejuvenating all my senses. Our meetings were unique, I thought. Externally, nothing seemed to happen; but with each encounter, our sense of intimacy deepened.

I was shocked by the strength of my feelings. I tried

to stop thinking about Mark with all the willpower I possessed, but he dominated my thoughts. I had been brought up to distrust men, and my marriage had only reinforced this. But Mark's simplicity and sincerity soon disarmed me, and I found myself trusting him completely.

For a long while, I was reluctant to define the nature of my feelings for him. I just like talking to him and laughing with him, I tried to convince myself. But as the days went by, I could not deny it any longer. It had happened. I had signed my heart away and now there was no turning back. When I could finally accept this fact, I started to enjoy the sensations that this love gave me in my most unguarded moments.

I felt a strange sense of pride that these years with Divakar had not made me lose my identity. My marriage, which structured my existence, seemed so unreal and unimportant in comparison with the love that I felt for Mark. This free choice to love was the first independent decision I had ever made. The rest of my destiny had been decided by my parents; all my emotions were ones which others had told me I should feel. This love was born spontaneously in my mind. When I thought of Mark, I did not have to pretend. I felt free, as if my heart was soaring weightlessly into the skies. I began to have my own aspirations. I did not intend to remain Divakar's handmaiden. For the first time, I began to get a sense of my own life and choices, and to feel that it was possible for me to change my life. To dream once more when I thought I had lost the capacity amidst my torture was a beautiful form of escape. Falling in love with Mark was finding myself; to an extent I was not even that concerned about his feelings towards me. I knew that he found me attractive, and that was enough. I was married, so there was no question of him reciprocating; but that did not bother me. After five years of marriage, I was finally in love.

Yet sometimes I would realize the ugly way in which society would view my love. I had always viewed extra-marital relationships as demeaning. I was raised to believe that a woman should have only one man in her life, however bad he might be. In my sheltered life, I had not encountered too many women who had dared to flout that convention, but I had sometimes heard my mother and aunts talked guardedly of such women.

The only person I knew who had dared to defy such norms was Gowri, a maidservant in my mother's house. I was a child then. She was about thirty, with sparkling eyes and a smooth rounded body. I thought she was beautiful, and was amazed to find out that she had seven children; the eldest son, Puran, was twelve. She was a hard worker and would work at our house from six in the morning to late at night. She had to support the family because her husband, a dhobi, was a chronic drunkard. About once a week he would be sober enough to park his mobile wooden ironing cart under the neem tree at the corner of the street and stoically iron clothes with his coal iron box. On other days, Puran would light the coals on an iron grate and fan them continuously, sending scarlet sparks flying into the air. But few people wanted to trust their clothes to such a small child. When Gowri's husband was drunk, he would beat up his wife and children, so Gowri would often come to work with a bruised face or a black eye. Amma always tried to help her with medicines and food, and occasionally even call the dhobi over to reprimand him. But the abuse continued.

Gowri would often talk to the other servants, most often, though, to Sundar, the gardener. The two of them would work with Amma in her much-loved vegetable patch. Gowri's boisterous laughter would ring through the backyard, along with Sundar's low rumble. The other servants gossiped that Gowri was seen at the cinema with Sundar. Gowri started to look more cheerful and wore new brightly-coloured saris to work.

One day, neither Gowri nor Sundar turned up for work. After Appa left for work, Amma went to the front gate and searched for Gowri's husband or Puran under the neem tree. But the little cart was not there, and neither of them could be seen. By noon, the servants had decided that Gowri had eloped with Sundar. Amma sat pensively with her chin cupped in her palms. Around four in the afternoon, the dhobi was at our door, lamenting loudly and beating his forehead with his fists. Amma asked him to tell her what had happened. But I think she knew the answer even before he told her. Gowri had taken all her children and eloped with Sundar.

I could see that Amma was shocked, but she tried to calm him. 'She has gone and we cannot stop her. Sometimes, such things that are beyond our control happen. We have to be brave.'

He roared, 'I will not let her be! I will find her and cut up her evil body.' He pulled out his sickle.

Amma was flustered. She stood up anxiously and tried to talk to him, but he did not listen and stormed out of the compound, shouting obscenities. Amma walked back into the house, her face pensive and brooding. She telephoned Appa and asked him if he could have the dhobi arrested. Appa asked her to stop interfering in the lives of the menials and think of other things.

When I awoke the next morning, I could sense that something was wrong. The servants were huddled together in corners, whispering cautiously. Amma was weeping silently into her sari. Gowri's husband had found her and chopped off her head. He had then paraded himself with the severed head in his hand. The police had arrested him. He had not been flustered but stated calmly that he had committed the murder to teach other women a lesson. Most of the servants agreed with the dhobi. They declared that he was an honourable man and that Gowri had brought it upon herself. I knew that Amma did not agree. She walked to the vegetable patch and tenderly touched the plants she, Gowri and Sundar had so lovingly tended.

Because I had been a child when this happened, the incident made a deep impact upon me. And so I tried to guard myself against Mark's charm by pretending that I was impervious. I was also truly frightened. I had grown up in a cloistered culture, where the only men I knew well were my father and Divakar. And I had never imagined that I would love a man other than my husband. Even in my unhappiest moment with Divakar, I had never dreamt of falling in love with another man; I had just thought that I would never have the opportunity to love a man.

As I thought about my dilemma over and over again,

I wondered if Mark realized what kind of person I was. I knew that if I allowed myself to love him, it would be for good. And I knew that I would be satisfied only if I was loved equally intensely. Perhaps he thought that I was just a happy-go-lucky girl out to have a good time. But his disposition was too serious for him to indulge in something frivolous and passing; there was a candour and honesty in his eyes that suggested that he was incapable of deception. I felt that he would never take advantage of a vulnerable woman.

There were sweetly alarming occasions when he accidentally caught me staring at him. When his fingers unwittingly brushed mine, I would catch my breath in sheer wonder. I had never learned to take pleasure in my body. When my breasts first began to grow, I had felt only embarrassment and guilt, and had tried to camouflage them under ill-fitting garments. My mother and aunts whispered that soon I would become a woman. They warned me to be careful about men, and my curfews became stricter.

I remember the day I had my first period. I must have been thirteen. My classmate Savita had told me that girls who stared at boys often bled to death. It was on Deepavali, and I was making kili kolams with bright green parakeet patterns, wearing my new purple silk skirt. Suddenly, I felt a stab of pain in the pit of my stomach and realized that there was a dampness in my underwear. When I went to the bathroom to check, I was shocked to find a crimson patch, like a paan stain, on the white fabric of my panty. I froze with terror. Only yesterday I had secretly admired the new boy at the ice-cream parlour where I had gone with Amma to buy a chocolate bar. He looked at me interestedly, and when his fingers had brushed mine, I had blushed to the roots of my hair. I felt horrible now, for I thought that the gods had cursed me for my sin and I was going to bleed to death. I sat in the bathroom for what felt like hours, tears streaming down my cheeks. I was afraid to tell Amma, for then she would find out that I had flirted yesterday. It was well past lunch hour, and the smell of food wafted to my hungry nostrils. Finally I heard Amma calling me, telling me she had made my favourite murungakkai sambhar and fried eggplant, and that it was all getting cold. I responded by bawling loudly. When she came to me, I told her about my condition. Surprisingly, she did not punish me, but hugged me.

'You have become a big girl,' she told me. 'Go and wait in the bathroom outside.'

This was the bright and sweet-smelling bathroom near the well in the backyard. It was reserved for the elaborate Friday baths when Amma washed our hair with egg white, shikakai and reetha. I sat there and waited, looking at the water which the sunlight stealing in through the blue glass windowpanes had turned a brilliant azure. Amma bathed me, pouring cool water on my shivering body and rubbed freshly-ground turmeric into my skin. She washed and dried my hair. She told me that this was an important day in my life, and that I was lucky that I had attained womanhood on a day when the stars were in their best places in the firmament. I was very confused. Amma had reacted as if she had expected this to happen to me. I wondered if Savita had lied.

The room farthest from the puja room was washed and emptied of furniture for me. Amma said that I had to stay there for ten days before I could come out. I was made to sit on the floor and eat out of a separate plate. Amma dressed me in a peacock-blue silk sari with a red border. I complied quietly, hating the fact that what was happening to my body had become so public. There was a ceremony to which my parents invited all their friends. In our community, cousins called moraimappilais are considered the natural suitors for a girl. When a girl attains puberty, these cousins are supposed to weave coconut palm leaves into a filigree-like wall. My seven moraimappilais each made a section of this leafy partition which was arranged like an enclosure around me so that it was as though I sat in a thatched room. This symbolized that the men in the family were volunteering to build a home for this woman. I felt mortified as I sat there, watching them giggling as they wove the partitions. They commented slyly about how pretty I looked, and argued amongst themselves about who would marry me. I did not want to marry any of them, for they were bullies and boring.

Soon after, Amma gave away all my frocks. I could wear only long skirts and a half-sari. Every month, like the other menstruating women, for those five days, I ate from a separate plate and was barred from the puja room. My childhood suddenly seemed to have ended. My family's attention to the changes in my body made me feel ashamed of the external signs of puberty. Amma told me not to jump or run any more, and I believed that if I did, I would start menstruating again. I would continuously check the back of my skirt to see if I had soiled it. This fear transformed me from an active child into a silent woman. As my body changed, I grew more and more ashamed of it and what it could do. My mother reiterated that I should keep my eyes lowered when I spoke to men. She told me horrifying tales of bad girls getting pregnant and delivering monsters.

When I was growing up, there was only one time that I had a glimpse of the pleasures of womanhood. Rahul was six years older than I was, and he was my father's best friend's son. That was why he was one of the few young men allowed into the inner quarters of our house. My mother adored him and considered him the son she never had. My friends were all infatuated with him and envied me because he used to visit regularly to help me with my arithmetic.

One day when Rahul was teaching me algebra, he took my fingers in his and softly remarked, 'Aradhana, you are growing into a real beauty.' I was shocked but I felt a strange wave of pleasure sweep over me. I pulled away my hand hastily. He looked embarrassed. Soon after, he went away to Chennai to become a doctor. I never saw him again.

By the time I had come to terms with growing up, I was married off to Divakar and our marriage did nothing to allow me to take pleasure in myself or my body. It was only after I met Mark, that I began to feel that my body was beautiful and that my spirit was free again. When I had visited Pattiamma's house as a child, I would run to the bamboo grove nearby while she and Amma were sleeping in the hot afternoons, lie down in the cool shade and close my eyes. Bees made holes in the bamboo trees, and the breeze blowing through these made beautiful music. I would just lie there, listening, until I heard Amma calling me back to the house. Meeting Mark was like the beautiful interludes I had had in the bamboo groves of my childhood, like resting in cool shade after the scorching blast of the sun.

SEVEN

Before I met Mark, I had one friend in Darjeeling. Her name was Gayatri. She was also from Tamil Nadu, and I enjoyed speaking Tamil with her, which few people in Darjeeling spoke. I got to talk to her about domestic things too: of Kancheepuram silks, Pongal, and the singers S.P. Balasubramaniam and K.J. Yesudas. She showed me where the south Indian rice and spice shops were, and gave me prasadam which her many relatives brought her from Tirupathi and Thiruthani. She and her husband Ramesh were childless, but they had a happy and loving relationship. She took me under her wing soon after we met and became like a big sister to me. She was the only person who listened compassionately when I told her about the horror of my married life. She was very supportive, yet she knew as well as I did about the impossibility of doing anything about it.

I had met Gayatri at the somewhat unlikely setting of a Tuesday kitty party at the President Club, which was one of the ritual social obligations that Divakar forced upon me. It was not exactly exciting to sit and gossip with the other wives of Divakar's acquaintances, but he wanted me to get to know the wives of his important business associates. The women of varying ages—similar only in that they were the bored wives of rich men—would turn up in their best clothes. We would spend a full hour talking about each other's clothes, after which came the character assassination, which was invariably dominated by the sharp-tongued Mrs Chaudhury who had a new juicy tale for every Tuesday. Then would follow a lavish lunch after which we would disperse for siesta.

I remember vividly the day that I told Gayatri about Mark. I had just acknowledged to myself that I was in love with Mark, and that my life was starting to turn green and alive like the grass that emerges after the first rains. Gayatri had invited me over to have lunch and to see her daffodils. I was in high spirits because Divakar was away on a two-day business trip to Hyderabad. The daffodils were indeed lovely, in full bloom like my spirits. The sun fell on us with gentle warmth as we sat in the patio to eat. It was spring and the world was dazzlingly beautiful.

Gayatri noticed my exuberance. She looked at me suddenly, 'Aradhana, you look radiant. Has there been an improvement in your relationship with Divakar?'

I was surprised. Was it that obvious? I looked down at my napkin. 'Well, I am just happy, Gayatri.'

'No, there is more. Tell me, Aradhana. There is something different about you today.'

'Well, Divakar has a new friend, Mark. He is Canadian . . .' I stopped.

Gayatri's big kohl-rimmed eyes widened with interest. 'So?'

'He is . . . very nice to me, Gayatri.' I suddenly felt that it was okay to tell her. 'I like him.'

'Aradhana!' She was shocked. 'Are you telling me that you are in love?'

I realized that she might misunderstand what I had said. 'Gayatri, I am not having an affair with him. I simply like him.'

But Gayatri was still concerned. She wanted to know what kind of a man he was, and whether he was in love with me. I realized that I did not have the answers myself. I looked blindly at a pair of brilliantly-coloured Monarch butterflies dance in amorous unison amidst brilliant flowers. 'Gayatri, I simply know that I love him and that I am happy. I don't know much else.' She didn't say anything more but hugged me warmly and I felt immeasurably reassured.

All these uncertain feelings crystallized and settled into certainty one evening when Mark had a party at his house. It was a wonderful evening. As was usual at such parties, men and women formed separate groups. As the evening wore on, I started to get bored with the inane chatter of the women around me. I toyed with the slim stalk of my glass of juice and scanned the crowd for Divakar to see if he showed any signs of wanting to leave. I saw him deep in conversation with a group of business associates. Mark saw me looking around and must have sensed my acute boredom. He came and sat down beside me. I was surprised but I did not show it. I smiled at him, then averted my eyes to look out of the window.

'Aradhana, are you doing okay?'

'I am fine.' I nervously fingered the peacock motif on my turquoise blue sari.

'That is beautiful.'

'Thank you. It is hand-embroidered,' I said almost inaudibly.

'Did you do it?' he asked, gently caressing the fabric with his fingers. I nodded.

'You are so talented!' he spoke softly.

'Do you remember the huge wall painting in the foyer in our house? I painted that too.'

'That's so beautiful! Did you go to art school?'

'No, but I did a course in Tanjore painting. A kind of home-study programme.' I looked at the bare walls of his house. 'You should put something on these walls.' I looked at him. His gaze wandered over the walls and came back to meet mine. 'Perhaps I should paint something for you—a bright picture to highlight that wall.' I walked over to the centre of the big bare wall in front. 'Right here, I think. I could do a nice painting . . .' I looked at his furniture, taking in the hues. 'Something in green, red and yellow . . . Actually something in basic earth colours would look beautiful.'

He had walked over to me and was standing very close. I could feel his warm breath fall on my shoulders. Suddenly I ran out of words. He was silent too. I turned to look at him and saw a strange expression on his face. I don't know how long we stayed that way, unaware of the world around us. It was blissful. Strange sensations coursed through my veins. I don't know if he felt it too, but at that moment, I felt sure that he did. Intense joy seemed to blend into my body with the supple ease of soft clay swirling on a potter's wheel. It was very new but it felt very familiar to me. That one moment was so complete in itself.

When I went home that night, I took out my easel and set up my canvas. He had filled my mind with the colours of spring, and now I spilled them onto the canvas for him. The delicate contours of a woman's form flowed from my fingers with no conscious thought. I felt as I had when I was a happy girl rushing through the paddy fields. I liked this sense of release, the naked poetry that wafted from my heart. But as I put the last strokes on the canvas, an icy sensation enveloped my heart. I was falling in love with a man who was not my husband. It had sounded easy when I confided in Gayatri, but now I felt a growing fear.

The following day, Divakar told me that he had to go to Germany for a week on work. I was elated, but I tried not to show it as I packed his business suits and organized his briefcase. I breathed a sigh of relief as he walked out of the door. I called Mark and, for the first time, actually arranged to meet him at the mall at six. I dressed carefully in a pale blue sari and brushed my hair till it was silk. When I looked at myself in the mirror, I knew I looked beautiful. I took the painting that I had done for him with me. I asked the chauffeur to drop me off at the mall. The five-minute drive seemed like an eternity. I sent the car back home after telling Ramu that I had a lot of chores.

I gave him the rest of the day off.

Mark arrived five minutes later. 'Yes?' he said, his eyes laughing into mine. 'And why do you need to see me urgently?' I gave him the painting without saying a word. He just stared at it with awe and reverence. After a few minutes, he looked up. 'Aradhana, it is beautiful. I can't tell you how much this means to me.' He broke off and rubbed his hand across his eyes. 'Let's go to my car. I need to sit down.'

We got into his car and he sat simply gazing at the painting. After a while, he put an arm around me and hugged me. 'Aradhana,' he said, 'thank you. The painting is wonderful. No one has ever done something like this for me before.'

I could not say anything. My heart was so full that I had no words.

'Why don't you talk to me? Do I bore you?'

I knew he was teasing. So I laughed happily and complied. 'There is nothing to say about me. Tell me about yourself. How come you are so gorgeous and still single? Why did all those lovely girls in Canada not grab you?'

'Well, actually they did. But they liked it better when I grabbed them back.' He winked mischievously. I felt a hot flush creeping under my skin.

He reached out and touched my chin tenderly. 'Is your modesty outraged, Aradhana?'

We started to laugh. I had never laughed so genuinely or so unabashedly with anyone before. I paused momentarily to look at him and found him staring into my face with such tenderness that it made me want to hug him. And I did just that.

Finally he broke the blissful silence. 'I think we should find a better place than a parking lot, don't you agree?'

I nodded happily.

'Where would you like to go?'

'Mark, as long as I am with you, the place doesn't matter,' I said softly. I simply wanted to savour every moment of being together. I needed nothing else.

'Well, then maybe we should go to my place. Would you like that?'

I nodded and he chuckled softly.

I felt an enormous sense of peace walking into his house. Though I had been there before, this was the first time I was alone with him. I walked around and looked at all his little things, small in themselves, but a part of his life; things that he had put together. I exulted in the sensation of getting to know him better. Everything was unique because it belonged to him. I felt instantly at home, and very comfortable.

He hung up the painting and I felt proud that I was now a part of his home. I stood staring at it, thinking how right it looked on his wall. I was so absorbed that I did not hear him come up softly behind me. I felt his kiss fall like a feather upon my shoulder. A rush of sweetness filled my mind. I turned to face him and saw intense tenderness in his eyes. When he kissed me, it seemed totally right and completely natural.

He made supper for me. When I offered to cook, he refused gently. In my community, men never cooked. Apart from professional cooks, he was the first man who had cooked for me, and I was filled with wonder as he moved dextrously around the kitchen.

I slowly walked up to him, leaned gently against his back and closed my eyes. 'Mark,' I whispered softly, 'I love you so much.'

He turned, held me close and kissed my forehead.

'Am I doing something wrong? Mark, will I go to hell for this?' I asked him.

'Of course not. My god would not find you guilty; no god would. It is okay to feel this way.' He kissed me again and added, 'I think you know yourself that this is normal, don't you, Aradhana?'

I did not answer. The evening passed in quiet enchantment, and then he dropped me home. When he drove away, my heart felt strangely light. It was as though he would always be with me in spirit; that I would never be alone again.

I did not see Mark for the remaining few days before Divakar returned. I was wrapped in a haze of delight, and was content only to think and dream about him. The future of our love did not bother me. I felt immensely privileged that I had been given the chance to really love a man and be loved by him.

Then Divakar returned. 'What have you been doing with yourself?' he asked me.

'Oh, nothing much,' I replied. He looked angry.

'You don't seem happy to see me.' He went over to the bar and poured himself a drink. Then he walked towards me. 'Have you been seeing Mark?' I moved away in reflex. 'Did you have a nice time with him? Was he finally able to take your so-called virginity?' He caught my hair in a vice-like grip.

I felt that familiar fear creep into me. I braced myself for his next move.

'Answer me, you whore! Was it good? Did you do it in my bed or did you go to some seedy hotel? Answer me, you slut.' He forced some of his drink into my mouth.

I felt nausea rise. 'I don't know what you're talking about,' I said as steadily as I could.

'Of course you do! Your escapade with him must have been quite memorable. Tell me.' He struck my face with his glass, cutting my cheek. The alcohol seared the raw wound.

'Why do you think I slept with him, Divakar?'

'Ramu told me that you went to meet him. You are a fool, Aradhana. Do you think I would let you stay here unwatched? All my servants report to me. Now everybody knows that Divakar's wife is a common slut. Tell me the truth. Did you spread your legs for that bastard?' He slapped me again.

I knew that it would be disastrous for Divakar to find out about Mark and me, so I forced myself to remain calm. 'Yes, I went to meet him but nothing like that happened. You know that I had offered to do a painting for his house. I took that to him. I did it for him only because he was your friend.' I cast around desperately to find arguments that would appeal to him. 'Divakar,' I said, 'how could a married woman like me be interested in another man? My mother raised me well. You know I will never bring shame on this family or my father's family.'

That seemed to pacify him. Every time I proved to

him that I was the properly brought up woman he had married, he was satisfied.

It was Friday and I started to fill little lamps with oil and put wicks in them. But inside, I was still frightened. When I lit the lamps, my hand trembled. He was smoking nearby and he noticed that. He came close to me. 'Why is your hand trembling, Aradhana? Are you lying to me?' His voice sounded menacingly low.

I felt a shiver of fear. 'No, there is nothing to lie about,' I said shakily.

He grabbed my hair and knocked me onto the floor. 'Divakar, why do you hit me?'

He laughed, as I lay sprawled on the floor. 'Aradhana, I can never trust you. All women have treacherous minds. But I trust Mark. He is a decent man; he would not want a whore like you.' He grabbed my left foot and pressed the burning end of his cigarette on it. I screamed in pain and pulled my foot away. 'This is to warn you not to have plans of running away.' He laughed again and walked off.

In bed that night, I thought of Mark's gentleness. The pain in my body seemed to evaporate instantly, and I managed to fall asleep.

But the next morning, I could not get out of bed. My face was bruised, swollen and purple. The burn in my foot throbbed excruciatingly. I lay there, drained of all willpower to move. At some time in the late afternoon, the ring of the telephone penetrated my haze of pain. I picked up the receiver.

It was Mark. 'I love you, Aradhana,' he said softly into the phone.

I almost dropped the receiver. 'Are you still there?'

'Aradhana, I love you,' he repeated the statement as if to reinforce it.

'Mark . . .' I could say no more. I said his name over and over again. I sat there, feeling incredibly happy but weeping copiously. When I managed to stop crying, I told him about the previous night's events. He was completely shocked because I had never told him about the sufferings I underwent in my marriage. We spoke for hours and finally, I put down the telephone reluctantly. I had spent these years with Divakar's indifference, which made me feel asexual and unloved. To have someone like Mark care what happened to me made me feel like a complete woman, cherished and alive. He gave me back the femininity that my marriage had stolen from me. It was like coming of age all over again; only this time, there was no stigma attached.

The sun was setting in the western sky, and the horizon was glowing with the warm colours of fire. The sunset sky in Darjeeling is a delight. But even that brilliant kaleidoscope was nothing compared to the warm hues flooding my mind. I looked at my body with renewed wonder. For the first time in my life, I was thrilled to be a woman.

E I G H T

Loving Mark gave me inner strength. Previously, I had passively accepted Divakar's embráces so that sex was over as quickly and painlessly as possible. But now I felt I belonged to Mark and no other man should touch me. I fought Divakar in bed when he reached for me. Divakar always managed to overpower me, and I would lie there, my resolve to leave him, strengthening.

While Mark and I could not meet often, we talked regularly on the telephone. Our sense of commitment and trust grew, and our mutual need deepened. I don't know how matters would have been resolved had things carried on this way.

Around this time, however, life took one of its most unexpected and bizarre turns. I discovered that I had missed my period. In my absorption with Mark, I had failed to notice for several days that I was overdue. I was a bit worried, but I knew that I could not be pregnant, for our sexual relations continued to be incomplete. When I contacted Gayatri and told her about my predicament, she arranged for an appointment with her gynaecologist immediately. As I went for the tests, I tried to reassure myself that I was not pregnant, could not be pregnant. There was a mistake somewhere. My marriage wasn't even consummated. How could I be pregnant? It all seemed impossible. But I became more and more terrified.

I sat stonily in the gynaecologist's office waiting for the results. Gayatri held my hand tightly in hers. The gynaecologist's words shattered my fragile composure.

'Congratulations, Aradhana. You are going to become a mother.'

I felt my head reeling. 'Doctor,' I said, 'I need to talk to you.'

'Of course,' she said reassuringly. 'All mothers-to-be have lots of questions. Go ahead.'

I don't think she was expecting what was coming, though. I told her about my sex life with Divakar; that I was still a virgin. She tried to hide her surprise and examined me to check that I was not mistaken. The examination confirmed that my hymen was intact.

'Aradhana, I am really sad that you have lived like this for five years. Have you and your husband talked about this?'

I told her how Divakar blamed me for being frigid and sexually deformed.

She shook her head. 'None of this is your fault, my child. There is nothing wrong with your body. You are going to be a mother. It is a miracle, but nevertheless, the truth. A woman can get pregnant if a man deposits semen even externally on her genitals.'

Her words sent shivers down my spine. I did not want to bear Divakar's child. My life had suddenly become full of happiness and hope, but now it seemed to be falling to pieces around me. I wondered dully why God picked me out to perform his medical miracle on. And why now? It was ironical that I was carrying one man's child in my womb and another man's image in my heart. If I had borne a child earlier, Divakar might have been less abusive. I might have become reconciled to my marriage. But now, my impending motherhood seemed to signal the death knell of the new dreams of freedom that my love for Mark had given me. There was no way out of this marriage now. I was doomed. I knew Mark was in love with me, and I felt I had betrayed him by getting pregnant by another man. This child, unwanted by me, fathered by a man I hated, was ending all my hopes of happiness and forcing me back into a marriage that I realized I had already decided subconsciously to end.

Gayatri understood my confused feelings before I even articulated them fully. We both knew that having an abortion done in a nursing home would be out of the question, for then, Divakar would definitely come to know. We would have to approach some midwife who did illegal abortions. Gayatri warned me that this would be very dangerous for me. Deaths resulting from such abortions—usually carried out by untrained and illiterate women in their slum dwellings—were only too common. But I was so determined to terminate the pregnancy that I was prepared to take any risk. After much persuasion, Gayatri agreed to make the necessary inquiries on my behalf. She found out about an old woman who did such abortions. I knew I had to go through with this and resolutely tried not to think about it.

The next morning, Gayatri picked me up from my house on the pretext of taking me to the temple. We drove to a dusty village about thirty-five minutes from where I lived. We parked the car at a distance and started to walk down the dust-swept mud track. It was not easy to find her house, but we finally managed to do so and knocked apprehensively on the wooden door.

A thin woman in her seventies with snowy hair opened it. Her witch-like countenance had as many wrinkles and folds as the earth itself. She had huge paan-stained teeth, and a dirty brown sari covered her tiny frame. She seemed to know why we were there and let us in without a word. The room was thick with smoke from a burning wood stove on which a pot of rice and fish sat cooking, and it was crammed with pots and pans and clothes. My eyes watered from the grey acrid smoke. It took my eyes a few minutes to get adapted to the dimness. She asked us to sit on the only piece of furniture—a bamboo cot. I began to feel nauseous. Gayatri asked her how she carried out abortions. The woman showed us an iron prong. 'It is very simple,' she said. 'I heat this prong and put it on her lower abdomen. That will kill the child.' She laughed, showing broken teeth. I shuddered in terror. Yet I was determined to lose this baby.

'Do it,' I said, much to Gayatri's consternation. I lay down on the bed and undid my sari to reveal my stomach. The woman put the iron prong into the wooden stove on which the pot was sitting and waited for it to heat. She came to me and wiped my brow.

'I will give you a salve made out of several herbs to apply on the blister,' she said. 'It will heal in about twenty days.'

I nodded silently. It all seemed logical but completely surreal. I was cold but sweating profusely. I could feel the thin sheet on the cot clinging to me. I heard her pick up the now red-hot prong from the stove. I was petrified. I knew that the pain would be excruciating beyond imagination. I opened my mouth to scream but my voice was strangled in my throat. As she came near me, holding the prong, I heard Gayatri scream, 'Stop!' The woman froze.

I sat up and looked at Gayatri gratefully. We both knew with great clarity that this was not how it should be. I quickly covered my stomach. We apologized to the woman, paid her the fee and left the house. It took me a long time to stop trembling.

Gayatri too, was severely shaken. 'Aradhana,' she said slowly, 'sometimes we cannot prevent fate. We have to accept it. It is too dangerous to go in for that kind of abortion.'

Death seemed a happy solution but I knew I could not kill my child like that. With a feeling of cold despair, I realized that I now had to give birth to Divakar's child. I reached my house in a daze and went to my room. I looked at my body with growing distaste. I put my palm on my stomach. It felt strangely different. I sat down on the huge bed and cried till my tears ran dry. Now I was bound to Divakar forever.

When Divakar came home that evening, I told him

that I was pregnant. He looked at me with a mixture of disbelief and absolute delight. 'So you are not sterile after all; just frigid. I am going to have a son. I hope he looks like me. How long have you been pregnant?' He looked at me with triumph in his eyes. I hated to have given him this victory.

'About a month,' I said looking down at the carpet.

He went off exultantly to call his mother and tell her the news. I knew it was just the beginning of the celebration. He would announce my pregnancy to friends and family in great style, because to him, it was a confirmation of his manhood. I cringed as I thought of all the years ahead with him, mothering his baby. I felt as if I had lent out my body for some alien visitation.

I went upstairs slowly and snuggled beneath the covers. I wanted to be as insignificant as possible. I could never be alone again. It was now that I had truly lost my single identity. For nine months I would have to hold a part of Divakar constantly inside my body. I started to cry softly into my pillow. Mark was drifting further and further away from my life. I thought of the happy hours of the last few months, which now seemed so unreal. The heartache mounted with every passing minute. I wondered why after five years of barrenness, my body had suddenly become fruitful. I had read somewhere that a woman is more likely to become pregnant when she is happy. My spirits had soared because of Mark. But ironically my womb opened to Divakar, and it was his child I was pregnant with. I felt absolutely cheated. There was nothing I could do. Just as I had scented freedom, my prison had become still more fortified; and with a child, I was truly trapped.

My desolation grew as the months passed. Darjeeling was turning chilly. The sun rose later; there were fewer birds and their song was plaintive, and the butterflies had all but disappeared. By early November, when I was four months pregnant, I was content to spend all day snuggled under my blankets, reading romantic novels. My only outings were my periodic visits to the gynaecologist and Divakar never accompanied me.

Divakar still had his huge weekly parties, but he did not mind if I excused myself. Since I had discovered I was pregnant, I had not met Mark even once, or talked to him. I avoided him because I felt I had betrayed him. And somewhere, obscurely, I felt that he had let me down too. He must have heard about my pregnancy from Divakar, but he had not called me either. I could not bear to see him but I still thought obsessively about him.

One day at breakfast, I casually asked Divakar whether he would like a son or a daughter. He looked surprised. 'A son, of course. A son to carry on my heritage. You know, Aradhana, I really appreciate the fact that you are pregnant.' For once, he appeared content.

I felt a sudden urge to break his complacence. 'What if it is a girl?'

'A girl? Well . . .' he cocked an eyebrow. 'No, no, of course it'll be a boy. No man wants a daughter.' He leaned over and patted my left arm as if to reassure himself.

'But Mark said once that all men want to have daughters,' I said testily.

'Oh Mark!' he laughed aloud. 'You see, Aradhana, these white people do not know the value of a son. Todd, that guy from the US, keeps raving about his four daughters all the time. He ought to be ashamed that he could not produce a son even after four attempts.' He laughed again with genuine pleasure.

'Maybe he did not actually want a boy. Actually, Divakar, I would love to have a daughter.' My fervour surprised me.

He was instantly at my side. 'Aradhana, don't say inauspicious things. Anyway, you should not worry yourself. Not at a time like this.'

I was tempted to ask him what he meant by worry, but I let the matter go. I started to pray for a daughter and even started knitting a pink bootie. After almost six years of passive obedience, I felt that giving birth to a daughter would be my ultimate weapon to crush Divakar.

Then one magical day, I felt the first movement in my womb, a little nudge in the secret lake that had sprung within my body. It felt strange to hold something within me; something that was part of the man I hated, yet felt was all mine. Something told me that it was a girl. I began to wonder what she would look like. Would she have my eyes and hair or would she shock me by inheriting her father's stern features? I placed a tentative palm on my stomach. She would be a miniature image of strong womanhood. She had decided to grow within me at a certain moment. Maybe she wanted to break my solitude and give me company. I wondered how much she could see and feel of the world outside; whether she was frightened when she heard Divakar's thundering voice; whether her little heart skipped a beat when he touched my body brutally; whether she felt the coarseness of the raw silk sari I was wearing. I looked out of the window; rain was starting to fall. Could she smell the rain too? Would she be a rain girl like me? Strange, she was created of the seed of the man I despised— I felt so tender towards her. I wondered if my thoughts would reach out to her and create in her a character that would not submit to oppressive forces.

I felt very close to my mother, now that I was going to have a daughter too. She and Appa were so delighted at the news. Amma told me to eat a lot of spicy pickles. As I put a dot of mango pickle on the tip of my tongue, I wondered if my daughter would feel the tangy taste as it travelled through the umbilical cord into her body. Amma also instructed me to eat blanched almonds and saffron flowers to ensure that the baby was fair. She sent me little balls made of some ten types of pulses ground together with jaggery and pure ghee. I looked at the pale green sweet-smelling balls arranged in the round steel container like a pyramid. I could see her sitting on the kitchen floor, tightly squeezing the powdered stuff into perfect little globes. I picked one up in my hand; the rest of them shuffled to rearrange themselves in the container. The imprints of her fingers on it felt like touching my mother's palm.

Each day the baby grew inside me. As the day when I would become a mother drew closer, I became more of a daughter. I constantly remembered my life with my mother. Memories of those days encircled me until I felt I myself was in a womb created by them. In that strange half-trance state, I progressed to motherhood. My stomach swelled silently and my skin developed a translucence of its own. Where I had earlier thought my baby would take away my individual state, she seemed to make me more complete within myself.

I thought of Mark in the midst of all this. Though I had not seen him for months, it still felt as if he were watching me transform from one being into two. I could visualize my baby in his arms. That seemed more natural than imagining Divakar being a loving father. Mark was inside my heart, inside my body. I felt that my daughter must know him already.

I wanted my daughter to have a loving father who would spend time with her. I had grown up wondering why my father never carried me, and why he never told me stories. I knew he loved to talk; when my uncles came to visit, they would hang on to his words. But with me he was always silent. He would smile at me sometimes when he saw me on the swing. Sometimes I would talk loudly to my dolls just to get his attention. When he lifted his head from the files he was always busy with and looked at me, I would lower my head with a burst of shyness. I loved the way he smelt—a combination of Brylcreem, Colgate toothpaste, Cinthol soap and tobacco. When Amma cleaned Appa's room, I would pick up his discarded shirts and hold them to my nose. It almost felt like hugging Appa. I doubted very much whether Divakar would give my daughter the kind of attention I had craved from my father, and I felt a twinge of sadness that my daughter would never have a real father either.

In the seventh month when I went to the gynaecologist, I was a bit worried because I was feeling short of breath. There seemed to be a heaviness every time I inhaled.

But she reassured me. 'It is normal to feel breathless. It's nothing. The baby is growing; she is moving closer to your heart,' she said. I smiled. She was right. My daughter was moving closer to my heart in more ways than one.

As the due date drew near, I became more dependent on Gayatri. She was the person who attended to my every need. When in early April the time came for me to go to the hospital, she was the person who accompanied me. I had to have a Caesarean, and I was given a caudal anaesthetic for my surgery. That meant that I was awake during the operation. When I heard the doctor say, 'It's a girl!' my elation was complete. Divakar came over to the hospital during the operation but he left soon after. I saw the doctor giving him the baby. I heard him tell Gayatri how disappointed his parents would be that it was a girl, and I knew that he must be deeply distressed too. I also heard him tell her that he had to go to Tokyo for a week. I went to sleep happily, knowing that he would be gone when I awoke.

When I woke up after many long hours, my hospital room was filled with pink balloons and flowers. And there was Mark in a chair by my bed, his face tranquil and relaxed in sleep. A day's stubble darkened his chin. I looked at him for a long moment. It was such a pleasure just to see him after so many months that I was content to just gaze at him and felt reluctant to wake him. Finally, I called his name. His eyes fluttered open and he was instantly at my bedside. He pushed away a lock of hair from my forehead and sat down beside me.

There was so much of pent-up longing to express that I could not speak and tears welled up. I felt a deep sense of loss in that I could never belong to him now that I had a daughter. 'Mark, I am really sorry,' I said finally.

'Why, Aradhana? I will always love you. The baby is a part of you. It does not make me think of you any differently. I love you more than ever. You should trust me.'

I cried uncontrollably then, with joy and relief. He kissed the top of my head and smiled. 'Hey, Aradhana, I saw the baby. She is gorgeous.' I was delighted that someone else other than me appreciated my baby.

Divakar returned with a lot of baby things for Tanya. He even picked her up and cuddled her a little. But his interest lasted only a while and he soon returned to his total absorption with his work. He would stop by her nursery, once in the morning and once at night, but there was nothing of the playful exuberance or keen interest that one expects of a new father. He was reluctant to even pick her up, but he did shower her with gifts. I wished my baby had a father who did not mind his shirt being creased or dribbled upon. I knew that Divakar would be a remote father like mine had been.

When I got home from the hospital, my daughter was finally all my own. In hospital, the nurses had kept her away from me apart from at feeding times. I looked at my daughter with renewed wonder. I could not believe that so much perfection could arise from something so imperfect as my union with Divakar. That soft smell of milk and baby powder wafted up to me like a gossamer embrace. Her incredibly soft skin felt like a caress upon mine. I gazed amazed into her huge black eyes within thick lashes; at the perfection of her tiny nose. The tug of her gums on my nipples as she suckled was painful and ecstatic.

Even within the first days, I realized that having a daughter had changed me forever. I realized that I did not want for Tanya the life that I had had. And because I had borne her within me for nine months, I felt an immense sense of protection. It was my responsibility to protect her from all those who would thrust her into the kind of life that had been ordained for me. I would not let the web that surrounded me entrap my daughter. I wanted her to grow up without inhibitions, to enjoy her feminine nature and her body. For the first time in my life, I held within my hands the responsibility of someone else's happiness and I was determined that I would not allow anyone or anything to mar her growing up.

NINE

Tanya changed my life. The monotony and emptiness that I had associated with Darjeeling, except in the brief period after Mark entered my life, disappeared. My days were wrapped up in taking care of her, dreaming dreams for her. Motherhood changed everything.

Yet a part of me still longed for Mark's calls. With Tanya, I had to be strong and protective. With Mark, I could be an equal, be cherished myself. I could talk to him in a way I could not talk to anyone else. After I came back from the hospital, we spoke regularly on the telephone and I realized that our love was still as strong as it had been. Meeting was out of the question, and these intimate telephone sessions were the only possible interaction. I felt I was blossoming every day with Mark and Tanya in my life. I started writing poetry and listening to music. I felt a sudden zest for life, and a deep enjoyment of everything around me.

Divakar knew that I was talking to Mark regularly.

And because I knew that the servants he had set to spy on me would tell him anyway, I decided to tell him myself. I knew Mark was a prospective client, representative of a wealthy foreign company, and Divakar still wanted to impress him and recruit him for his own firm. So he allowed me to talk with him over the phone when Mark called, ostensibly to ask me about recipes and local artisans. But I had an uneasy feeling that this state of calm would not last long. And my foreboding was soon justified.

One day when Mark called at his usual hour, Divakar was still in the house though I did not know it. I picked up the phone and said 'Hello, Mark' gaily, even before he had spoken. Suddenly my wrist was caught in an iron grip, and the receiver was wrenched out of my hand and slammed down.

I felt Divakar's palm land on my right cheek in a resounding slap. 'I don't want you to talk to Mark so often, do you understand? What is it that you two talk about for so long? He is going to think that you are waiting to tumble into bed with him, you whore.'

My eyes blurred with pain and shock. Divakar had not hit me or tried to have sex with me since I had told him I was pregnant, and I had even begun to hope that the physical abuse would not start again. I started to walk slowly back to my room, my head throbbing. But Divakar grabbed me, pushed me to the floor and crouched over me. For a second I was almost afraid that he would kill me. He removed his belt and started to beat me, the lashes on my body creating welts as they fell. The pain sent me into spasms. I could hear Tanya bawling in the background.

I dimly heard him stomp out of the room and slam the door after him. I felt a wave of nausea as I dragged myself to the bathroom. I retched uncontrollably, tears streaming down my face. I cried for the miserable life I had, for all my thwarted dreams, and for the fact that I did not even have the right to protect my own body. I picked up my wide-eyed daughter and held her close to me. I cried helplessly because I had brought her into such an ugly world. My determination to protect her hardened. I knew that there was a world out there, very different from the one I lived in, and I knew I had to find it for my daughter. I did not know when and I did not know how I would find it, but I only knew that find it I would. I had to.

It was only that day that I really became aware of the intensity of my problems. My mother had told me that a woman should be like a basil plant: pure, holy and quietly residing in the backyard of a house. And that was the ideal of purity and subservience I had tried to live up to. That day, I decided that this ideal had lost its validity. I started to dream of freedom again, but this time with a firmer sense of resolve because now my daughter was involved too.

Mark called me the next morning to find out what had happened because I had abruptly disconnected the phone. He knew enough about my life to make a fair guess. Much as I wanted to talk to him, I had not called him that morning because I knew that he would be deeply grieved if he heard the sorry tale. I had resolved not to tell him, but when I heard his voice, my sense of pain and outrage made me blurt out the truth. I could feel him wince with shock even over the telephone. He told me how inadequate he felt in that he could not protect me. He wanted me to leave Divakar immediately. I explained to him that that was not such a simple matter. Despite the fact that this was incomprehensible in his background and culture, he understood. He did not call me a coward but supported me simply and totally.

Despite the complexity that this had led to, I was so grateful to God that Mark had come into my life. I had thought of myself as a woman incapable of real love. Now I felt like a real woman, and I loved that feeling. It seemed so natural to love and want the touch of a man. My religion decreed that women should live lives of silence and patience. These were the values my mother had instilled in me. I found all those beliefs slowly fading from my mind. I forgot the dictates of my religion and prayed fervently to God to give me Mark. In that one moment of revelation, I realized how desperately I wanted our love to succeed. 'Oh God!' I whispered, 'you led me to Mark; don't take him away from me. Please don't.'

But I was also concerned that because of me he might be exposed to harm. I was afraid that Divakar would try to harm him or even murder him. After all, murdering one's wife's lover was not uncommon. Maybe I should never have loved Mark. He was a bachelor from Canada, from a world I did not know, and he was on the threshold of an exciting career. I was married; I just had too much baggage attached to me. I felt that I was a burden to him. I hated my present life, and I hated myself for loving Mark. It seemed that I was being selfish in doing so; that I should set him free. Yet all I wanted was to be in his arms.

After a long night of thought, I decided that I should get out of Mark's life. I told myself that I was doing it for him. I started avoiding his phone calls. Divakar noticed this. He seemed pleased; he must have thought he had taught me a lesson. What helped me to stick to my resolve was that it was now time for us to take Tanya, aged three months, to my parents' house for the traditional ear-piercing ceremony. I had not seen my parents since I had become pregnant, and I was eager to see them. They too were anxious to see their first grandchild. My mother-in-law had sent my mother a long list of gifts and jewellery that she had to buy for Tanya as well as for Divakar and me. Divakar decided that Tanya and I should go a week before him, as my parents wanted to take us to various temples that he had no desire to visit. I did not tell Mark that I was leaving him. I packed my bags enthusiastically, hoping that this act would sever all ties with Divakar.

The journey to Madurai was quite a tedious one. I had to take a train to Calcutta and then fly to Chennai. From Chennai, it was another six-hour journey by train. I was exhausted but excited. My father was there at the railway station to greet me. He immediately took my gurgling daughter from my arms, and gave me a warm smile. We drove to the house in happy silence. Amma was waiting on the porch, beaming. I was overjoyed to be home as I took in the familiar smells of that huge, old house.

The next day, my mother casually asked me why Divakar hadn't accompanied me. I was expecting this question. In our community, if a married daughter returned home without her husband even for a holiday, it could signify only one thing: the marriage was on the rocks. I put a piece of dosa into my mouth. 'Amma,' I began, 'he is busy, and you know that we are not exactly a very happy couple.'

She was shocked. 'Aradhana, don't talk like that. We wives have to adjust. You have a child now. Remember that. You have a happy marriage. Your husband earns a lot and you have a child. Divakar is a nice boy. You have to be patient.' She peered anxiously into my face. I carried on eating in silence.

My mother did not bring up the subject of my marriage again, and I did not pursue it. Amma believed that if a problem was ignored long enough, it would disappear. And I wanted to enjoy my stay at home.

I decided to spend my days of freedom before Divakar arrived visiting friends and relatives whom I would not have time to see once I got caught up with rituals after his arrival. One of the friends I wanted to see was Deepa, who had recently returned to Madurai. She had married a wealthy doctor shortly after my wedding; my mother had said it was an excellent match. I was happy to hear that, as Deepa was a joyous person with huge eyes always filled with mirth and lips curved in an impish grin. It was hard to imagine her other than laughing. But when I went with Tanya to Deepa's house, I had difficulty recognizing her. She looked old and grim. On seeing me, her eyes momentarily filled with the old sparkle and her lips stretched in a wan smile. She picked up Tanya and led me upstairs to her room. As she lived in a joint family, this was the only place where we could have any privacy. Once we were alone, we started to talk.

The tale she had to narrate was horrifying. Her husband was abusive, demanded money from her father constantly and beat her mercilessly if she confronted him. There was no way she could leave the marriage as she had a three-year-old son and was now pregnant again. There was nothing I could say to comfort her, and I felt again the futility of the lives our loving parents forced us to live. I did not tell Deepa anything about my life. I felt she had enough to bear. As I was leaving, she said, 'Aradhana, I don't know how long I can go on like this. I feel like ending it all.' Her words shocked me. I had thought that my married life was unique in its horror.

Divakar came the next week. The ceremony and the ear-piercing ritual for Tanya were held that Friday. Velusamy, our family goldsmith, was to do the piercing. Amma dressed Tanya in a little red blouse and yellow skirt with a red border. There were little bangles and chains adorning her neck, arms and feet. There were elaborate gifts for my mother-in-law, Divakar and me. Tanya was placed in the lap of a male cousin of mine, as per custom, her ears pierced with a thin gold needle and two tiny red rubies inserted. She was put in the sandalwood cradle after that, where she fell asleep happily as my mother sang lullabies to her. Divakar was satisfied with the ceremony because it had been very ostentatious and had obviously cost my parents a small fortune.

We were to travel back to Darjeeling on Sunday morning. I spent the last day at home shopping with my mother. This was always fun because we giggled together and behaved like little girls. We went to the famous Haneefa silk store, drank fresh sugarcane juice and bought glass bangles by the yard. I also picked up gifts for my friends in Darjeeling: a blue chungudi sari for Gayatri and a bronze Krishna for Mark. When I packed my bags, I hid the Krishna at the bottom. Despite all my resolutions, I thought of Mark with longing, and the thought of seeing him again made the prospect of leaving home and returning to Darjeeling much easier.

Mark called soon after we got back and I agreed to see him because I wanted to tell him I had decided never to see him again. He invited me to his house. I took him the statue of Krishna and an old edition of a book we both loved which I had found in an old bookshop in Madurai, James Mitchner's *Sayonara*. A certain thoughtfulness and stillness overshadowed the joyous expression with which he had greeted me when he saw the gifts. We sat down in the patio and he looked intently at me.

'Aradhana,' he said quietly, 'is *Sayonara* just a casual gift or is there something more to it?'

'Mark,' I began as best as I could. 'Mark, I need to go away from you. It is better that way.' There was a tightness in my throat which made it difficult for me to speak.

'Better for whom?'

'For you,' I said and stopped.

'And what made you think that you know what is best for me?' There was decided anger in his voice. 'Aradhana, do you honestly think that you are the one who can decide whether I can share my life with you?' He stopped as if too hurt to continue.

'Mark, I think that it is time for me to get out of your

life,' I said with all the courage I could muster.

'Aradhana, don't you realize that though you seem docile, you are actually violating my rights? You are stepping into my private zone and telling me how to feel. You decided for me that I should forget you, and you're destroying my freedom of choice. What makes you think that I can forget your love? You might think that Hanayo in *Sayonara* is noble, don't you? No, Aradhana, she too was selfish, just as you are—selfish and totally unconcerned about the feelings of the man.' He took my hand in his strong clasp and stroked my fingers. He looked up at me and our eyes locked.

I lowered my eyes away from the intensity of his. 'Mark, Hanayo did what she had to do to ensure that Grover had a peaceful life. She did not want to disrupt the calm order of his existence.'

His hurt look stopped me. 'Grover says that he loved everything about her—even the dust from the strokes of her broom mesmerized him.' He paused and ran tired fingers through his brown hair. 'Tell me, do you honestly think that what she did was a good thing, that Grover appreciated what she did? No, she stole from him what he desired the most. Her sense of nobility was totally misplaced.' Then he looked into my eyes intently. 'Are you going to do me the same injustice?'

We sat in silence and then he asked me again, very softly, 'Is this your reward for my love? You are the first person with whom I have been so totally honest. Are you going to make me regret this closeness we have shared by destroying all my trust? If you want to walk away, don't justify it as concern for me.'

He was right. I had made decisions for him without considering his feelings. That day at his house, I realized the honesty and intensity of his feelings. And this rare spiritual honesty with which he treated me made me realize that I could not live without him.

T E N

My life settled back into a reasonably tranquil pattern after we came back from Madurai. Divakar now believed that I was totally under his control, and so his need to assert his power over me was much less. Tanya was growing into an enchanting child and I was conscientious in ensuring she had a joyous childhood. There was always Gayatri, who loved to spend time with Tanya and sing to her and talk to her. And then there was Mark, who brought perfect joy and peace into my life. Divakar seemed to have become reconciled to the fact that we talked on the phone and when we met at the frequent parties.

But one evening when I was reading in bed, Divakar entered looking furious. My body instinctively braced itself for his attack. He pulled all the bedclothes off until I was shivering in the cold of the evening. He stripped my clothes off in grim silence. He then sat opposite me and stared at my naked body, still not having uttered a word. My teeth chattered and I pulled my long hair around me, for warmth, as well as to shield myself from his gaze. He moved swiftly then, leaping across the room to grab a pair of scissors. He caught my hair in a vicious grip and snipped it off close to the roots, occasionally jabbing the blades into my scalp which started bleeding. In the cold, I could feel the hot blood drip down. I sat frozen in silent horror as he worked on in complete silence.

Finally, he threw down the scissors and said quietly, 'I have to go away on business again. I want to make sure that your lily-livered lover will not want to see you. You look like an ugly hag now. No one could possibly want you.' He slammed the door behind him as he left, and soon after, I heard the front door slam.

It took me almost three hours to move from the corner I was cowering in. I could not stop shaking. I finally managed to pull myself to the bathroom mirror, and peered at my reflection. My hair hung in disorderly clumps; at some places, there were bald patches. He was right. I did look grotesque now.

I remembered what Divakar had said about Mark. Strangely, I did not feel ashamed to see him even in my devastated state. I realized that I wanted intensely to see him. Without thinking any further about it, I took a cab and went to his house. I did not even bother to check if he was home. I rang his doorbell anxiously. When he saw me, his expression was one of absolute shock. He let me in and took a long moment to shut the door. I knew that he needed that moment before he could face me again.

He took me in his arms. 'What happened, Aradhana?

Why did he do this to you?'

I buried my face in his chest and started to cry. I sobbed for a long, long time. I told him what Divakar had said and done. He listened in silence.

'Where is that bastard now?' he asked tersely.

'Oh, he left . . . Mark, look what he did to me.' I held a wisp of my remaining hair in my fingers and looked at him through tear-filled eyes.

He caught my fingers in his own. 'You are still beautiful, Aradhana. It would take much more than that to take away your beauty.' He carried me to his bedroom and sat me on his bed gently. He turned the lights down so that only the pale white moonlight filled the room. He made me lie down and leaned over me. He kissed my brow, my nose, and then covered my lips with his own. I felt my body quiver and melt as he moved on top of me. I looked up into his eyes and caught the fire in them. He undressed me like a prayer, kissing my body and leaving a burning trail of passion wherever his lips and fingers touched. I felt myself respond instinctively, in a way I had not imagined possible. Finally we were naked, and the lean contours of his body moulded with the soft curves of my own. He touched me with a gentleness that took away all my inhibitions and fears. His hardness against me created an intense desire to feel him inside my body; the sheer force of this desire almost frightened me.

He caught fear in my eyes and paused. 'Aradhana, I won't hurt you, I promise. I will stop if you want me to. Would you like me to?' He kissed my eyes softly. I responded by seeking his lips with my own. That kiss became more passionate as I started to move in unison with him. Then his pace quickened and he was moving gently inside me. I could see the shock in his eyes as he met the barrier of virginity. There was a momentary pain; then pleasure and passion took over.

I had never thought that sex could feel good. I was filled with joy and a feeling of being blessed that the man to initiate me into the wonder of making love—of making me feel like a true woman—was this wonderful man whom I loved.

'I love you, I love you, my precious,' he repeated softly and gathered me into his arms. I closed my eyes blissfully. We lay there together in each other's arms and time stood still around us. I had never felt more beautiful before. All life's problems seemed so trivial. I looked at his face in the shallow light of the moon. He looked so relaxed in sleep. I was filled with a wave of love and I kissed him softly. He moaned my name in his sleep and snuggled closer.

He awoke after a while. 'Aradhana,' he said softly, 'are you all right?' He looked into my eyes. 'Are you okay? You were still a virgin—I don't understand. Did it hurt?' There was so much tenderness in his voice. In the deep privacy of his bed, I could cast away my inhibitions and explain the bizarre nature of my sex life with Divakar.

He kissed my brow after I finished and spoke with great firmness. 'Aradhana, you will have to leave him. There is no way I want you to go back to him now. You are mine. I cannot let him treat you badly again.' He sat up beside me. 'Aradhana, I have to go away to Canada. Will you come with me?'

Suddenly, the choice seemed very simple. 'Mark, if I

stay on here, my life will never change. My parents would never let me go back to them. I have nothing left for me here, and I don't want Tanya to lead the kind of life I have had to live. But I hate to do this to you. You deserve . . .'

'Aradhana, it is no longer your battle alone. It is our battle.' He took my fingers in his own. 'I want you and Tanya to come away with me. I need you in my life. I love you, my darling. I have never loved anyone like this.'

'Mark . . .' Suddenly what he had said about leaving, registered. 'Are you really leaving?'

'I have to, but you will come with me, won't you?' He stroked my hair gently.

I would have gone with him to the very end of the world if he had so wanted. My life now would be a void without him. I rested against his broad chest and he rocked me gently. I wanted the moment to last forever.

I went back home that night feeling like a different woman. I had broken all the taboos of my tradition, and felt enormously happy and liberated. I could not believe I had made love with a man other than my husband, and more amazingly, that I did not feel guilty about it. I felt none of the grief I felt every time Divakar touched me. It was like being born again. I wanted to leave Divakar now, with a fervour I had not thought myself capable of feeling. Now that I knew what it was to feel joy, I hated the monster who had made so many years of my life so miserable and taken away from me my dreams and every shred of self-respect.

I wanted desperately to talk to somebody, so I went

to see Gayatri the following morning. I had almost forgotten about my appearance in the joy that pervaded my being. It did not seem important any more. But when Gayatri saw me, she almost screamed. 'Aradhana, who did that to you?'

I did not have to answer that question.

'What did Mark say?' She automatically assumed that I would have confided in him. I did not look into her eyes. I was still afraid of her reaction.

'Gayatri,' I said softly, 'there is something that I have to tell you. Something really important. You must promise to forgive me if I was wrong.'

'Aradhana,' she stroked my hair gently, 'after Divakar did this to you, what could you possibly do that is wrong?'

'Gayatri, after this happened, I went to see Mark. I told him everything.' I focused on the richly-spun carpet. 'We ... we made love.' I stopped.

I could feel her body tense. 'Aradhana,' she drew me into her arms, 'if anyone is ever to blame, it is Divakar and not you.'

'He loves me. He wants me forever. What happened between us was simply an expression of our love. When he saw how Divakar had disfigured me, he wanted to show me that he would always find me attractive. It was not just sexual.' I looked at her. Gayatri was a chaste woman who had lived her life faithfully and dutifully according to the dictates of society. And yet I was telling her that I had had sex outside of marriage and she was accepting it without outrage.

'Aradhana,' she said, 'you cannot stay in this marriage

now. You have to leave. Just remember that it was for your own sake and your daughter's sake.'

I left her house feeling a great sense of relief. I knew I should leave India before Divakar returned. If I remained in India, he would hunt me down and try to thwart my happiness. And I could not trust my parents. They would only force me to go back to him. I knew that to them and to my clan, I would be a fallen woman, and ostracized. They would never, like Gayatri, try to see the reasons why I did what I did.

That evening, I went to see Mark again. We decided that the sooner we made our plans, the easier things would be for us. Time was our enemy. The first thing we had to do was to get a Canadian visa for Tanya and me. The only Canadian consulate in India that issued visas was in Delhi, so we decided to go to Delhi immediately. I contacted the embassy by phone to find out what documents I would need. I was informed that Tanya would need a separate passport. I felt a chill. To apply for a passport for Tanya was impossible because I would have to get Divakar to sign the form. We were devastated. Now our options were limited. I had to leave the house and file for divorce from within the country. I had a sense of amazement that I who had had all decisions, big and small, taken for me, was now taking such major decisions on my own.

Under the circumstances, the best possible way for me to proceed was to hide from Divakar for as long as I could. After a year of separation, I was eligible to file for divorce. Until then, I had to be as quiet as possible. The limitations of family law meant that it was virtually impossible to get a restraining order on an abusive husband. What I needed was a place where I had friends who would be able to help me.

As I was mulling over the options open to me, I suddenly thought of Ramola, Maya's childhood friend who used to come to our house and purloin my father's cigarettes. I knew that she had become a practising attorney. My mother and her parents, the Ramachandrans, were neighbours and good friends. Whenever I visited Madurai, Amma gave me news about Ramola. Ramola continued to shock her family and mine, but I think Amma had a secret affection for her. Ramola had topped her legal exams and become a well-known lawyer, noted for her work on women's issues at the famous legal firm of Ramakrishnan and Ramakrishnan in Chennai. She had also outraged her family by marrying a Muslim colleague of hers, who was an equally brilliant lawyer at the same firm. My mother had also told me, with a hint of disapproval in her voice, about a shelter for battered women that Ramola had started. She had recently won a national award for her work there and I had read about it in the papers. I also followed her column in the Tamil magazine *Kumudhan*, with great interest.

I picked Chennai as the place I wanted to move to. I was sure Ramola would be the best person to help me. I knew she had had considerable affection for me. She had sent me a present and a warm letter when I had got married. Besides, Chennai had other advantages as well. It was far away from Darjeeling and I was familiar with the city. Moreover, it was a reasonably large and cosmopolitan city where I could live inconspicuously.

When I told Mark of my decision to move to Chennai, he was happy for me. Though he was sad that I would go away, he knew that I should find a place as far away from Divakar as possible. That was the important thing. I also felt that though this stay in Chennai was complicated, it would give me the opportunity to nurture my independence. Much as I loved Mark, I did not want to run away like a coward and be dependent on him. I wanted to be with him as an equal, not as someone he would always be obliged to take care of.

It had been only three days since Divakar had left, and we decided that Tanya and I should leave the following day. Mark offered to drive us to Calcutta. From there we would fly to Chennai. We decided to buy tickets under false names so that Divakar could not check the reservation lists and locate me. Mark also wanted to stay to help me settle down in Chennai. I was touched by the way in which he wanted to share the responsibility for my life and take care of me.

I planned my departure carefully. I did not want to excite the suspicions of the servants. I packed one small bag. I was very fortunate that I had enough money in the bank to cover my expenses for a few months at least. At around three in the afternoon, I slipped out with Tanya and took a cab to Mark's house. He was waiting by his car.

We had a long night's drive ahead of us, down from the mountains into the plains of West Bengal to crowded Calcutta. As I sat beside him once more in his little black car where so many of my dreams had begun, I realized that this journey was unique in that I was embarking on a new part of my life. I leaned back and closed my eyes. I had never thought my freedom would come so soon.

Despite the many weary hours, that drive was such a joy. We laughed and talked all through the night. Every so often Mark would reach over and ruffle my hair or squeeze my shoulder. These simple gestures were so important to me because I had never known that they existed.

We reached Calcutta as dawn was breaking the following morning. We stayed at the Taj Bengal, surrounded by green palms. I enjoyed the intimacy of checking into a hotel with him. We bathed and went to bed, despite the odd hour. We made love, and as I lay there in his arms, I was struck by desolation that he would be leaving me in Chennai and going back to Darjeeling. I started to cry.

'Aradhana, what's wrong?'

'Mark, I just thought that once we reach Chennai you will have to go back. I just began to miss you suddenly.'

'It is only for a short while, my darling. I am going to miss you so much too. There is nothing I want more than you living with me, my love. I know that we have to wait for a while. But one day not very far off from now, you will be with me as my wife.'

That evening we took the flight from Calcutta to Chennai. Being in Chennai felt a bit more like home terrain. Tanya was tired but cheerful. She was clinging to Mark and refusing to come to me. We checked into a hotel and decided to start hunting for an apartment the following day. As I went to sleep that night in Mark's arms, I felt so immensely safe and cherished in the circle of love we had created.

ELEVEN

We were up at six to pore over the rental columns in the Hindu and make a list of the places we thought might be suitable. We phoned the landlords and made appointments. The first apartment we went to see was a two-bedroom flat in Besant Nagar. The landlord, a short serious-looking man in his early forties, was almost unctuous as he showed us around the apartment. It was clean and new, the rent was low, and the balcony had an excellent view of the beach. Mark looked inquiringly at me, and I nodded happily.

'We would like to take this please,' Mark told the landlord.

'Who will be taking the house?' he asked, looking from Mark to me.

'I will be living here with my daughter,' I said.

'Where is your husband?' he asked.

I could see that Mark was irritated by that question. He moved to one of the windows and pretended to look out.

'Well, only I and my daughter will be moving in,' I answered as politely as I could.

'Are you a widow? No, you cannot be,' he said, looking hard at the bindi on my forehead.

'No, I am not. Now can we talk about the lease please?' I asked him.

'I cannot lease it out to you,' he said.

Mark was at my side instantly. 'What is the problem?' he asked.

'Sir, this is a respectable building. We have to follow certain principles. I cannot rent it out to her. She does not have a husband and she is not a widow. The other families would object if I leased it out to such a person.' He opened the door and waited for us to leave.

I saw Mark's jaw clench and I knew that he was about to say something. I clasped his fingers in my own to restrain him though my eyes were smarting with angry tears. I had never even begun to think that it could be difficult for a woman to rent an apartment alone. I was being made to feel I had transgressed some major social rules, though in my heart I knew I was not guilty. I felt defeated at this setback so early in my new life. Mark put his arm around my shoulders as we walked out. I could feel the eyes of the landlord boring into my back.

I looked at Mark with tear-filled eyes.

'Aradhana, don't worry. Don't take this man's comments to heart. We'll find something,' he tried to cheer me up. I walked quietly to the car. This was my first experience of trying to live as a separated wife and mother, and I was still reeling under the blow.

A woman owned the next apartment we went to see.

She was in her fifties and quite elegant. She seemed enthusiastic about a white man renting her apartment; perhaps she was hoping for a higher rent. I was happy because I thought a woman would probably have no qualms about having me as her tenant. But this hope was short-lived. As soon as we came to the question of signing the lease and she was told that I would be living there with Tanya, her enthusiasm waned.

'Do you mean that the gentleman is not your husband?' she looked aghast.

Mark and I exchanged glances. 'Well, no,' I said.

'Where is your husband then?'

'Well, I don't live with him any more,' I said as nonchalantly as I could.

'Are you married?' she glanced at Tanya.

'I was,' I said patiently.

'Is there a problem with that?' Mark was exasperated. 'She pays the advance and she signs the lease. Is it mandatory that she has to have a husband?'

'We don't lease our places to fallen women. We are religious people; we want only pure women to stay in our houses. No decent building will rent to a single woman, especially one who comes with her boyfriend to look at the place. What is the world coming to? Shiva, Shiva!'

When we were back in the car, I cried uncontrollably. I had heard enough for one day. I was already tired of the whole thing. Back in the hotel, we sat for a while in dejected silence.

Finally, Mark spoke with resolution. 'Aradhana, there is only one thing to do. I should sign the lease and you can stay there. Let's do that, okay?' He took me in his arms. 'It will all be fine. All these hurdles can be crossed.' I rested against his chest, wondering how I would have survived without him.

He left Tanya and me in the hotel to rest while he went to look at the other places on our list. He was back in two hours with good news. He had leased a beautiful apartment by the beach in Besant Nagar, near the first apartment we had seen. I liked it immediately when I went to see it with him the following day. We spent the next couple of days joyously decorating the place. Those days were magical, filled with laughter and togetherness. We laughed at the same things, and because our tastes in books and music were very similar, we never ran out of conversation. We'd catch each other's eye in the middle of even a crowded shop and be instantly transported to a different private place.

It was a bright and sunny day, so we stopped by a roadside vendor selling dailies and fruits for some coconut water. After we finished the water and waited for the vendor to halve the coconuts so that we could eat the tender white flesh within, I glanced casually at one of the newspapers on his stall. I was shocked to see my own picture staring at me from the cover page. I must have gasped aloud, for Mark was at my side instantly, looking over my shoulder at the paper. Beneath the postcard-size photograph were the following lines:

'Missing from Darjeeling: Aradhana Divakar (age twenty-four, height five feet six inches, complexion medium) and daughter Tanya (age four months). Aradhana is mentally deranged and may be a threat to the child. Handsome reward awaits anybody providing information about this woman. Please call the following phone numbers to report.' There was a list of numbers, and below that, an abrupt change in tone: 'Aradhana, come back home. I love you and my daughter.' It was signed 'Your pining husband, Divakar.'

I felt numb as I read this. Mark quickly paid the vendor, and propelled Tanya and me into the car. I was frozen with fear. My tormentor was after me. I knew what he was trying to do. He was portraying me as mad so that he could get me back into his house. This time, completely under his control. It would be easy enough for him to pay some shady psychiatrist to get a medical certificate stating that I was a schizophrenic. I had heard of such cases, and that it was always very difficult to disprove such a certificate in a court of law. I had never thought this would happen to me.

Mark drove to the apartment without uttering a word. He looked very worried. I sat in the car in terrified silence. I felt like a hounded animal with a bloodthirsty predator after me. I could almost feel Divakar's breath on the nape of my neck. Once we reached home, I mechanically washed and changed Tanya, and put her in her playpen. Then I sat on the bed, still quiet with apprehension. Mark sat down beside me and held me close. 'Aradhana, we have to act quickly. We should have gotten in touch with Ramola sooner. I was just too happy to be spending time with you to remember that we have many things to sort out.'

We searched the telephone directory for her number. There was a Ramola Ahmed listed. I was elated. It had to be her. I dialled her number nervously. I wondered if she would still remember me.

When she answered the telephone, I recognized her voice immediately. It hadn't changed.

'I don't know whether you remember me but I am Aradhana, Maya's sister,' I said hesitantly.

She identified me instantly. 'Aradhana, that little girl with long, long hair. How are you?' She sounded really happy to hear my voice. I felt a lot better immediately.

'Well, Ramola, I'm fine. How are you? I heard that you are now married. I hope you're happy.'

'I am very happy, Aradhana. Ahmed is a wonderful man. But tell me about yourself. I heard through Maya that you married a very affluent man. How are you?'

This was the hard part. I started tentatively. 'Ramola, actually that is why I was calling you. My marriage is over. I want to file for divorce. My husband is a very violent man, and now that I have left him, he is pursuing me and I need legal protection.' I sounded incoherent even to myself.

But she seemed to understand me. 'Aradhana, I have to see you. Come to my office as soon as possible.' She gave me her address and we fixed an appointment for five that evening. She sounded very brisk and competent, as if she knew exactly what had to be done. I felt some of the weight on my shoulders lifting.

Her office was in a prominent building on Mount Road, and it was easy to locate. Mark left me there and took Tanya for a stroll. As soon as I walked into Ramola's elegant office, she came to me and hugged me warmly. It was amazing to see her in her official guise. We had both changed so much since we had last met.

We sat down, and I told Ramola all about Divakar and the last six years of my life. She listened to me with utmost sympathy, asking the occasional question. I gave her the paper in which I was advertised as missing.

She looked at it and smiled. 'Don't you worry about this, my dear. This is a common trick that men like Divakar often try. We'll deal with this easily enough. Men like him can flaunt their power and muscle only as long as women are silent. Once we raise our voices in protest, there is not very much they can do. As you know, Aradhana, I specialize in family law and I have seen so many men like him. Take care of yourself and do not succumb to parental or familial pressure. This is a personal war for you. I am really proud of your decision to leave him. It was very brave of you. Just keep fighting and we will come through. As for this,' she looked down at the newspaper in her hand, 'this can be dealt with immediately.'

She called the editor of the paper in which the advertisement had been published. She explained the situation and then listened quietly for a long time. It seemed a friendly enough conversation, but she looked thoughtful and said 'I see' at intervals. Finally, when she put down the phone, she smiled at me.

'Don't you worry, Aradhana. Raman, the editor, is a friend of mine. He says that the ad will not be printed again. But he also told me a bit about what is happening behind the scenes. He said that Divakar is a good friend of Vinay Kumar, the son of the chief minister.'

'Yes, I know him. He was at my wedding and I have

met him a couple of times since. He does business with Divakar,' I said numbly, remembering the handsome man who had sat next to Divakar when we got married.

'Yes, Raman said they were close friends and that is why the chief minister is tacitly behind Divakar. But we have friends too, and the power of the law is behind us, so you are fully protected. The police officers are hand-fed by politicians, and the politicians are hand-fed by the rich people of our country. That is India. Our democracy is created for people who can purchase it. And it is men that have monetary power. This is why women are suppressed. But we can fight it out. Once we enforce our rights and make it a public issue, these corrupt men will have nowhere to hide.' She walked up to me and hugged me tightly. 'We'll do it. Trust me!'

I thanked her. I really felt very encouraged by her.

As I was leaving her office, she said quietly, 'You know, Aradhana, I know it's really none of my business, but I think you should write to Maya. She loves you a lot, you know. She loves her parents too. It's funny that our society supports a man who rapes and abuses his wife, yet jeers at a woman who chooses another woman as her sexual partner. A woman of Maya's remarkable brilliance and independence is highly unlikely to fit into the role of a conventional submissive housewife. I supported her from the time she first started questioning her sexual orientation. I am proud that she is my friend. No one has the right to decide how somebody else should live his or her life. Anyway, take care, dear, we'll work it all out.'

Mark was waiting outside and smiled to see my exuberance as I walked out. I hugged him. 'Mark, she's a genius! I'm going to be all right!' He leaned over and kissed the top of my head. Things finally seemed to be falling into place.

T W E L V E

It was time for Mark to return to Darjeeling. He had been away for too long, and he had to get back to work. Also, because Divakar was now looking for me, we felt it was better if Mark was not in Chennai with me. I was worried that night, most of all about Divakar seeking revenge. It would probably not take him too long to figure out that Mark had assisted me in my escape, and I knew Divakar was perfectly capable of taking the law into his own hands. But Mark laughed at my fears. He assured me that even Divakar would not be foolish enough to mess with a foreign national.

I cooked him a meal that night. I had never realized that cooking could be such a delight. I chopped vegetables while he sat in the living room, glancing up at me ever so often. I would feel a rush of joy every time his gaze caught my own. He set the table while I finished cooking. Eating the meal we had prepared together felt so intimate, almost like making love.

I snuggled up to him as we lay in bed. My tears were dampening his bare chest. I did not want him to go. I thought how happy and laughter-filled the last few days had been despite all the problems we had had to face. I listened to his heart beating under my cheek. It was the only sound in the stillness of the night. He propped himself up, with an elbow on either side of me. 'Aradhana, you're going to be okay, aren't you? You'll be brave for me, won't you? I'll be thinking of you all the time, and I'll be back before you know it.' His words brought fresh tears to my eyes. 'Hush, my love, you must not cry. I'll call you every day.'

'Mark,' I said, 'how can I say goodbye to you? I'm going to miss you. I miss you already.'

He kissed me, then sat up, reached under the bed and took out a little box. He cradled me in his arms and opened it. The next moment he slipped a beautiful diamond ring onto my trembling finger. 'To my dearest, to my only one, to my everlasting love.' He raised my finger to his mouth and kissed it.

I did not know how to respond. I had never ever dreamt of this kind of romantic moment. He started to make love to me again in the soft light. I had never felt so complete and fulfilled in my life. Being naked in bed with him had the kind of spiritual sanctity which I had thought only religious experience brings. It was as though we were above the call of society and the norms of real life. It felt so perfect to feel his skin against mine. It was as if we had transcended the ordinary and reached a sublime level of peace.

When the time came for him to say goodbye, I felt

strangely calm. He kissed me lingeringly and then walked to the cab. He waved to me and then he was gone. I stared at the fading rear lights for a long time. It was as though the most vibrant part of me was leaving. I glanced at the ring on my finger which caught the sunlight. I walked back into my house as bravely as I could.

We had hired a full-time maid-cum-nanny—a girl of about twenty called Lakshmi. Tanya took to her immediately and that was a big relief for me. I knew it would take Mark at least a day to fly to Calcutta and then drive up to Darjeeling, but I still waited anxiously for his call. For the first time, I wondered what Divakar was up to. I could imagine him pacing up and down in fury, downing drink after drink. He must have called my parents by now, and I wondered if I should call them too. I felt like talking to my mother. But I knew that they would immediately inform Divakar of my whereabouts and he would come to get me. If I wanted to have freedom, I would have to bear the pain of solitude. At least there was Tanya, and Ramola's comforting presence only a telephone call away.

The insistent trill of the telephone broke my reverie. I picked it up hoping that it was Mark. It was Ramola. 'Hello, Aradhana, how are you?' She sounded cheerful.

'Oh, I'm fine, Ramola. How about you?' I was really happy to hear her voice.

'Aradhana, Raman just called me. Divakar is in Chennai. Come to my office as soon as possible. Take a cab and don't bring Tanya.' I felt a familiar chill creeping up my spine. Divakar was in town. I had expected this to happen, but not so soon.

I instructed Lakshmi to stay indoors with Tanya and keep the door locked. It was around seven in the evening and almost dark. I dressed hastily and took a cab to Ramola's office.

She looked worried but tried to reassure me. 'Well, your husband certainly got here fast! Raman called me, as I told you, and tipped me off that Divakar was in the chief minister's house. Actually, I should have guessed that because a couple of hours ago, I got a call from my boss, Mr Ramakrishnan. He said that the chief minister's secretary had just telephoned him to order him to find out your address from me. Mr Ramakrishnan said that I should supply the address because there is no point in antagonizing the chief minister as he could make life very unpleasant for our firm. Of course I refused. He called me again just before you got here. He said that he was very sorry to do this to me, but if I don't supply all the details about you within twenty-four hours, then he will be forced to sack me. He said he could not afford to disobey the chief minister's orders.'

'Ramola, that is horrible!' I cried out in anguish. I had not thought that I might jeopardize her career.

'These threats don't mean much. I am just concerned about you. Listen, Aradhana, I want you to be careful. Stay indoors, because they might want to kidnap you or threaten you. I am not saying this will happen, but it is always wise to take precautions. And it is pointless to involve the police because the commissioner is the government's lap dog.'

I must have looked petrified because she added lightly, 'Look, probably nothing will happen. But it is good to plan in advance.'

'Do you think they will suspend you?' I asked.

'Well, I think Mr Ramakrishnan is now fighting it out with his conscience. His integrity as a lawyer should not allow him to do this to me. On the other hand, it is true that the chief minister will indeed make life very unpleasant for him if he refuses to comply. I will not be calling him up. If confronted, I will refuse to let out any information.' Her eyes took on a steely glint. 'Ahmed and I have talked about this. We have many friends in the legal community. If Mr Ramakrishnan suspends me, we will contact the Law Society—both of us are on the committee there—and ask them to organize a strike to protest. I also talked to the chairman of Aurat Mandir Trust, Renuka Tiwari, and she said that she would extend public support to your case. Once the lawyers' strike is on, we'll give interviews to newspapers—Tamil ones like *Dinathanthi* and *Maalai Murasu*, as well as national newspapers like the *Hindu*. Even if the government and police are corrupt, the media—or at least some part of it—is still free and honest!' She reached across and patted my hand. 'Aradhana, if you feel lonely, you can always come to my home and stay with me.'

I was so touched by her kindness. She was risking her life and career to help me. My life seemed filled with very good people who were taking risks for me. But on the drive home after I left her, I was suddenly terrified. It seemed incredible that the machinery of government—the chief minister, the courts and the entire police force of Tamil Nadu—were involved in trying to prevent me from escaping from my husband. My decision to leave him was no longer a domestic matter; it had become a political affair. My head started to spin as I realized the enormity of the situation.

I checked anxiously on Tanya as soon as I got back home. She was fast asleep. Lakshmi was awake, watching some Tamil movie on television. I didn't feel like eating so I asked her to eat and lay down on my bed. I hadn't heard from Mark, and though I knew I probably would not until the next afternoon, the passing moments magnified the fear growing in my mind. Even in the air-conditioned room, I started to sweat. I got up, poured myself a glass of water and popped an aspirin. I had a thundering headache.

The ringing of the phone penetrated the silence of the night, and I picked it up cautiously. I said 'hello' faintly into the receiver. When I heard the response I almost dropped the phone. It was Mark.

Caught between intense worry and joy at hearing his voice, I started to cry into the phone. 'Oh Mark, where have you been? Are you all right? Is everything okay?' I rattled off question after question without giving him a chance to respond.

'I am fine, Aradhana. I just arrived in Calcutta. Are you all right? You sound nervous and frightened. Did anything happen?' he asked anxiously.

I told him everything that Ramola had told me. 'Mark, please be careful. Divakar is a very dangerous man and now he is playing very dirty politics. Oh Mark, can't you come back here?'

'Aradhana, don't worry about me. If I have the slightest suspicion that they are going to accost me, I will contact the Canadian consulate at New Delhi. It's you that I am concerned about. I don't want you in any kind of trouble. Just follow Ramola's instructions and be brave. I will come back to Chennai as soon as possible and be with you.' He paused for a while. I did not speak either.

And then he continued in that soft tone I had so grown to love. 'Aradhana, I miss you. I can't go to sleep because I just want you here with me.'

'Mark, I miss you so much. I can't sleep at all without you. I just want you here.'

'I love you, darling. I will be with you before you know it.'

I held on to the receiver long after he had hung up. It seemed I was still in contact with him as long as I held on to it. I fell asleep with the receiver in my hand.

THIRTEEN

I spent the following morning potting the plants Mark and I had bought earlier and arranging them on the balcony. It was the best way I could think of to ease the tension that was growing within me. I hoped that the little rosebuds would bloom by the time Mark came. It was noon when I finished and the balcony looked like a garden. It was a beautiful day. The sea shone in the distance like a huge sapphire, the sky was cloudless, and there was a gentle breeze. I decided reluctantly to let the outside world in and called Ramola.

'Aradhana,' she said, 'I have just received a call from Mr Ramakrishnan. My services are being terminated from 1 September. I have been charged with undermining the integrity of the firm by involving myself in your case. Apparently we are conspiring to malign an innocent man, and I am misguiding and corrupting you!' She sounded quite cheerful about it. I looked at the calendar on the wall. It was already 27 August.

I felt enormously guilty that I was the cause of her dismissal. I said hesitantly, 'Ramola, maybe you should drop my case. I do not want you to be harassed because of me.'

'Aradhana, this is not just your case any more. This is an issue that concerns all women. It is clearly the government that is putting pressure on the firm, and neither the government nor a law firm has the right to tell a woman to go back to her husband. I don't care about being sacked; neither does Ahmed. Many of the lawyers from the Law Society are going on strike from Monday because our freedom to represent the wronged is being tampered with. Nobody can interfere with your personal life. We will not let them touch you. Don't worry about me. In fact I am looking forward to this confrontation.'

The weekend passed quietly. On Monday morning when I looked at the local newspapers, the lawyers' strike was in the headlines. The version that the government and Mr Ramakrishnan were putting forward was that Ramola was taking advantage of a mentally deranged woman, and forcing me to leave my husband. There was also a paragraph that quoted Divakar's statement to the press. He stated that he was worried about me and my mental stability. He was also allegedly petrified about the safety and well-being of Tanya, who was in the hands of a madwoman and a lawyer who was only trying to exploit me in hopes of getting money. He made it sound almost as if Ramola and I had kidnapped Tanya! The Law Society spokesperson denied these allegations and said that the dismissal of Ramola was stifling the fundamental freedom of all Indian citizens.

Ahmed called me around eleven. 'Aradhana, I am sending a man called Hussain to your apartment. Pack the things that you need for the next few days and you, Tanya and Lakshmi come to our house with him. Ramola wants you to stay with us until the worst is over. Be ready to leave in about half an hour.'

I was not too surprised by this. Actually I was getting more and more nervous about staying in my own home. Political murders were not uncommon. I had heard of women who had been killed—cases that had been passed off as suicide. I packed quickly, and asked Lakshmi to get Tanya dressed.

When the doorbell rang, I opened the door anxiously though I knew it must be Hussain. A man of about twenty stood there.

'Namaste, madam, I am Hussain, Ahmed sahib sent me here. Are you ready to leave?'

I nodded, locked the house and followed him with Lakshmi and Tanya.

The roads were crowded as usual, and the car moved slowly through the irregular traffic. It took us about half an hour to reach Ramola's house. She was waiting there for me, looking as cheerful as usual, with an array of newspapers and journals in front of her. Every one of them had her in the headlines.

'You know, Aradhana, I have just had a brilliant idea. We should turn Divakar's weapon against him. He is using the media, so should we. We should have a press conference this afternoon. We should tell the press that you are here, and you should tell them your side of the story. It's high time you were heard. The country is going to polls in a couple of months, so the government will not want to antagonize the public at large. If all goes according to plan, the chief minister will advise Divakar to back off a little. That will give us time to settle the issue.'

She paused and held my hand reassuringly. 'Do you think you can talk to the press, Aradhana? Look at the state of women in our country. There are so many abused and battered women who never get a chance to speak out. You have a chance and I think you should seize it. I know it will be hard, but can you be brave enough for this?'

I felt inspired as she spoke to me; inspired realizing that this was a chance to do my small bit for all women who suffered in silence. 'Yes, Ramola, I can do it.'

She called several newspapers and told them that I was with her and ready to talk. The response was amazing. I was a bit alarmed by the huge number of journalists who turned up at her door in the next one hour.

It was very difficult to talk publicly about something so private, and initially I was hesitant and fumbling. Ramola sat with me and held my hand when my voice faltered. But as I talked, the noisy gathering grew quiet and many of the women had tears in their eyes. When it was over, I was emotionally drained and very tired. But I felt a sense of triumph. I had spoken out; this was my first direct confrontation with Divakar.

The next morning we had positive news. The lawyers' strike and my interview had paid off. Ramola received a call from Mr Ramakrishnan's secretary, telling her that her suspension had been revoked and that Mr Ramakrishnan would call her shortly. We breathed a sigh of relief—something was definitely happening in our favour.

That afternoon, Ramola took me to Aurat Mandir, the women's shelter she had set up with a few other women. It was a sprawling building with about twenty rooms that housed around fifty women. I met Renuka Tiwari, another highly courageous woman who had been fighting for oppressed women all her life. She had a wonderful radiance and strength which captivated me immediately. She showed me around. There was a separate wing for children. The respect and love that Renuka and Ramola commanded were obvious. They took me to meet the inmates, some of whom were poor, illiterate women mostly between twenty and forty, many bearing livid scars of abuse.

I went over to talk to one of the women who sat in a corner, sewing quietly. She was around twenty-three, and beautiful. The left side of her face was severely scarred and the eye socket was a gaping hole. I looked at her in horror. 'What happened to you?' I asked, trying to keep the shock from my voice.

'My husband,' she said simply.

I sat next to her in silence, and after a while she continued, 'I was fourteen when I was married and I had four daughters in four years. My husband was very angry with me because I could not produce a son. He beat me and asked me to go back to my father's house. But my father was too ashamed to keep me there so he sent me back to my husband. I went back and begged my husband to let me stay in his house as a servant. My husband agreed. He had married again. One day his new wife saw me lining my eyes with kohl. She immediately called my husband and told him that I was too proud. To please her, my husband poured acid on my face and threw me out on the streets. Some kind stranger brought me to this place.'

'Aradhana, this is just one case of many,' Ramola told me when I narrated this story to her later. 'There is a woman here whose husband poured boiling oil over her stomach when she was seven months pregnant.'

I was aghast. 'But why? Wasn't it his child too?'

'Well, they had obviously conducted a gender determination test and found out that it was a girl. Her husband and mother-in-law tied her to the bed and poured hot oil on her stomach.'

Every story I heard hit me with a renewed sense of shock. It was unimaginable that men who did all this were walking free. I was mentally and emotionally drained by the time we left.

The whole of the following week was full of good news. Mr Ramakrishnan called Ramola, apologized to her, and revoked her suspension from the firm. Raman, Ramola's editor friend, told us that the rumour was that the chief minister had asked Divakar to withdraw his complaint. On the first day of her reinstatement, Ramola filed my application for custody of Tanya. I returned to my own apartment feeling much safer than I had ever before.

My life seemed to finally be falling into some kind of shape. It was fabulous to have my very own place. I visited Aurat Mandir every day, and worked with the women and children there. Working there was fulfilling,

yet paradoxically opened my eyes up to the horrific lives
that women had to lead. The story which haunted me the
most was that of Megha, a beautiful girl of about thirteen.
Her mother had named her Megha, meaning 'rain-cloud',
because of her dark skin. Less affectionate nicknames had
included Kalia and Kallu. As a child, Megha was tired of
being called names and being unfairly compared to her
fair-skinned sisters. She prayed every day that her skin
would become lighter. Her woes were multiplied when
her father died when she was nine, and her mother left
her at her maternal uncle's house. Megha's uncle had
molested her, telling her that she would become fair if
she had sex with him. After about three years of repeated
sexual abuse, Megha had got pregnant. Her uncle had
acted as though he had never touched her, accused her of
being a slut and threw her out of the house. When Megha
had returned to her mother's house, she was accused of
slandering her uncle's reputation falsely and turned out.
Megha had lived on the streets for two months, scavenging
garbage cans for food and begging near temples, until in
despair she tried to kill herself by jumping in front of a
speeding car. She lost the baby but survived, and had
been brought to Aurat Mandir. Like many others with
similar stories, Megha was now slowly trying to weave
her life back together again. What I found remarkable
about these women—young, old, Muslim, Hindu,
Christian—was how they lived in such harmony and
what a great source of strength they were to each other.
It moved me deeply to see the inmates smile and bloom
in the secure environment of the institution.

And when I came back in the evenings, tired out,

Mark would talk to me on the phone. These nightly calls would soothe my exhausted mind. I eagerly waited for him to come to Chennai. Every day I looked at my little balcony and hoped that the flowers there would stay in bloom until Mark arrived. Tanya was settling down very well in her new surroundings, and everything seemed peaceful.

My idyll was shattered one morning. I was on the balcony, where the sunlight fell in dappled designs and sparrows chirped. When the phone rang, I ran in and picked it up eagerly. There was a silence in response to my cheery 'hello'. 'Hello?' I said again.

A hoarse voice burst into guttural invective. 'Listen, you bitch, don't think that you've won. Your battle has not even begun.' I dropped the receiver in fright, and began to shiver violently.

The phone rang again. I let it ring for a while but finally I had to pick it up. There was a moment of silence and then I heard the same voice again. 'Your kid is going to lie dead on the streets. You are going to get raped by ten men—you and that other bitch, Ramola. What both of you need is proper sex to put you in your place!'

I put the phone down. My ordeal was far from over. Divakar would now seek subversive ways of ruining my happiness. I stared at the phone for a long, long time. I had to call Ramola and tell her, but I was too frightened to touch the phone.

The doorbell rang. I sat still, completely unable to move. But the visitor at my doorstep was persistent. I waited in silence hoping whoever it was would go away. He began knocking in addition to ringing the bell. I pulled myself together and walked to the door. I looked out through the peephole, but I could see nothing. I opened the door a little bit; there was nobody there. I looked down at the mat. There was a brown package, the size of a loaf of bread, lying there. I did not dare to touch it. I got back into the house and locked the door. I dialled Ramola's number and told her about the parcel. She told me not to touch it and said that Ahmed would come over shortly. I waited. I had heard of bombs being left outside doors, and I was too frightened to move.

When Ahmed arrived, he had another man with him. The second man scanned the parcel to find out if it contained a bomb. We all heaved a sigh of relief when he detected nothing. Ahmed opened the parcel. It contained a photograph of Tanya, which had been lacerated with a blade. It was wrapped in a few of her frocks, stained red with something that looked like dried blood. There was also a note that said, 'The next parcel will contain Tanya's mutilated body.'

I looked at Ahmed, totally shocked. He seemed stunned too. Then he collected himself. 'Aradhana, this is just a threat. We will deal with this later. Just keep a close eye on Tanya and don't let her go out with Lakshmi.'

For hours after he had gone, I sat and cried. I was petrified. Visions of Tanya lying dead and mutilated flashed across my mind. I wanted Mark desperately; I wanted the security of his arms around my body. When I heard the doorbell, I felt the familiar chill again. I opened the door cautiously.

'Mark,' I almost screamed.

'Aradhana, I could not leave you alone here. I had to come back.'

We sat down and I told him everything that had happened. He held me tight and spoke into my hair. 'Aradhana, I will never leave you alone again.' We sat together for a long time, thinking of the turn our lives had taken, and the reality of the monstrous situation we were in slowly started to sink in.

FOURTEEN

I must have fallen asleep on the sofa. I woke up to the shrill ring of the telephone. Mark was still sleeping. I was about to pick it up, but then I remembered the previous night's events. The telephone looked ominous and my head throbbed dully. But the caller was persistent. So finally I picked up the receiver and waited without making a sound. My relief was enormous when I heard Ramola's voice at the other end. She was concerned about the previous night's events and wanted to talk to me. We decided to meet at the Woodlands café.

I told Lakshmi to keep Tanya indoors and scrawled a note for Mark to let him know of my plans. I took a cab to the café. Ramola was already waiting there, looking stunning. She was in the first trimester of her pregnancy, and she glowed with good health and happiness. She hugged me warmly. We sat down at a table in a corner. I told her of my fears about Tanya. She gave me some sound advice. She said the police was unreliable so I had to be very careful about all my movements. Divakar would probably lie low until the polls, but as soon as the elections were over, especially if the ruling party came back to power, he would start hounding me again.

By the time we got up to leave, it was well after lunchtime and the sky was dark with monsoon clouds. There was a smell of wet earth as we walked out of the café. Ramola offered to drive me home. We took the road along the beach to my apartment. Though it was a longer drive, there was very little traffic, and it was very beautiful on this brooding afternoon. We were on a deserted stretch when the car suddenly stalled. Cursing under her breath, Ramola tried to restart it. It spluttered but despite repeated attempts, refused to start. We looked around, but there was no one who could help us. To one side was the placid sea, on the other, some abandoned half-built apartment blocks. There seemed to be no construction workers around. We got out of the car and stood by the road. A splotch of rain fell on my shoulder. I hugged myself as the now-chilly wind permeated my clothes. There were no buses along this road, and the few passing vehicles we hailed ignored us.

Finally, a scarlet jeep pulled up. A tall man in jeans and a jacket got out and walked towards us. I felt relieved that someone had stopped, but at the same time there was a sensation of sickness in my stomach. I looked at Ramola; she looked nervous too.

'What happened to your car?' he asked in a rather coarse voice.

'Oh, it stalled,' Ramola answered, trying to smile.

'Let me have a look.' He opened the bonnet and

peered at the engine. In a moment he straightened up again. 'There's nothing I can do. I don't have a tool kit in my car. But I can give you a ride.' He paused, waiting for an answer.

I did not like the idea of taking a lift with this stranger. 'We're fine,' I assured him. Ramola and I looked at each other nervously.

'Actually, we're okay. We'll figure something out. Thank you for your offer,' she said with an air of assurance.

The man smirked oddly. 'You'd better get into the car, Mrs Divakar. And tell your friend not to disobey me.'

We were completely stunned to hear him say my name. We realized with a cold shiver that this was all planned; that someone had tampered with Ramola's car and was now confronting us. Divakar must have planned all this. I felt a moment's relief that Mark was in Chennai and with Tanya. At least she was safe. Fleetingly, I thought of attacking the man—after all there were two of us—but another equally burly man got slowly out of the car. 'Now come along quietly,' the first man pushed Ramola towards the car. I followed her. The second man bound our hands with spandex once we were in the car and got into the front seat.

That drive along the deserted beach road lasted an eternity. I stared blindly out of the window. Ramola looked fixedly ahead. She spoke to me just once, and told me to just do whatever I was told. 'Offering resistance will just antagonize them.'

Finally we drew up in front of an abandoned house. 'Get out,' the man ordered. We were led to a large dark room on the ground floor. There were only two wooden chairs against the wall. They tied us to the chairs and left without a word, locking the door behind them.

The windows were shut and the room was terribly hot. My wrists were bleeding where the spandex cut into them. I could see the fatigue and fear on Ramola's face. With a start I remembered that she was pregnant. I felt desperately guilty that she was undergoing all this because of me. I didn't know what to say. We could only sit and wonder what lay ahead. My mind was filled with images of Mark and Tanya. My body was aching and there was a deafening throb in my head. My throat was parched.

After what seemed like hours, the door creaked open. The two men from the car entered, along with a third man. I recognized him—he was Ganapathi, who worked for Divakar. My worst fears were confirmed.

They walked straight to Ramola, ignoring me. Ganapathi slapped her across the face. Her head jerked back.

'So you are the woman set out to destroy a good family. You bitch, you already defiled yourself and Hinduism by sleeping with a Muslim, now you are breaking up another family.' He ripped off the spandex from her arms.

'Stop it!' I begged. 'She is only my lawyer. This does not concern her.'

He looked at me derisively. 'Mrs Divakar, this does not concern you. Just shut up.'

It dawned on me that these were Divakar's paid mercenaries so of course he would have ordered them not to touch me. But Ramola—they must have been asked to torture Ramola in front of me.

'Leave her alone!' I tried again. 'She's pregnant!'

The moment I said it, I regretted having mentioned it.

'So you are carrying a half-breed brat inside you. Let me see what he looks like.' Ganapathi pulled her up and peeled off her sari in one swift movement.

What followed was so horrific that the memory of it will never leave me. Even now, if I think back, every detail is clear in my mind. It seemed everything was happening in sickening slow motion and I was powerless to stop it or to block out any detail as Ganapathi flung her to the floor and the others held her down. I could hear myself screaming at them to stop, but even my screams could not block out the sound of Ganapathi unzipping his pants. Ramola's scream as he covered her body with his, will forever linger in my ears. He raped her over and over again. When her screams stopped, one of the other men poured alcohol on her face to revive her. And then they carried on. I tried to intervene but felt angry hands pull me away. Then, something heavy hit my head.

When I opened my eyes, there was silence in the room. My hands were not bound. My head hurt intensely. I put a hand to my forehead and felt blood. To this day I do not know why they did not kill me. I presume they had left me there for dead. The room was empty and in the eerie half-light, Ramola lay crumpled and naked on the floor. I got up slowly and walked painfully over to her. I knelt down beside her. There were cigarette burn marks all over her body. A thick nylon rope was tied around her neck. Her thighs were stained with blood. I took her hand in mine and whispered her name. Her hand was cold and limp. She was dead.

FIFTEEN

I awoke with a dull ache in my head. I was in a bed in a white room. The smell of disinfectant filled my nostrils. I realized that I was in a hospital. I tried to lift my hand and winced sharply as pain hit me. There was a bottle of saline attached to my wrist. There was nobody else in the room. I reached out painfully for the bedside buzzer.

A thin stern-faced nurse appeared. 'Oh, you're awake,' she said. 'Let me call the doctor.'

The young doctor appeared and smiled warmly at me. 'Mrs Divakar, how nice to see you awake! You are going to be fine. Just don't worry.'

I knew that I had seen something terrible but I could not remember what it was. I felt lost and confused. The only thing I could think of was Tanya.

'Tanya, I want Tanya,' I begged feebly. 'And Mark. Where is Mark?'

'They are fine. They were all here until about an hour ago. Mark took her home to feed her. I'll call your house and ask them to come back here now that you are awake.'

I lay there, trying to think. And then it came back to me. Ramola. The image came flooding back. I remembered that room of terror, my finding her dead, then that long desolate run along the coast road until at last I had met a man walking his dog and hysterically asked him to call Mark, to call Ahmed. The images filled my brain and I felt myself falling into a bottomless chasm of horror. I started to scream uncontrollably; I cried loudly for Mark and Ahmed. Finally, the nurses pinned me to the bed and stuck a needle into my arm. I fell into the peace of a medically-induced trance.

The next few days were traumatic. I screamed and cried constantly for Ramola. My dreams were full of half-grown foetuses being pulled out of women, of women being raped and strangled. I had to be kept heavily sedated. Familiar faces flitted in and out, but I didn't know whether they belonged to my dreams or to reality. The few hours I was awake, I sat like a zombie. I did not want to eat or talk to anybody. I did not even want to see my daughter or Mark. I was frightened of everybody, even the nurses and the doctor. I kept asking the nurses to shut all the windows. Ahmed came to visit me. I begged him to forgive me for what had happened to Ramola. He tried to reassure me that I was not to blame. But I was inconsolable, and I could not stop crying. Once I even begged the nurses to call the police station and ask them to arrest Divakar. After a few days—I don't know how many—the doctor decided to go easy on the sedatives. I was sitting, wide awake. It was midnight. Mark was half asleep in a chair. He woke with a start when he heard me say his name. He took me in his arms while I sobbed convulsively. I had wanted him so badly over the past couple of days, but I was also ashamed to enjoy the comfort of his presence. I felt guilty for Ramola's death and felt I had no right to have Mark in my life, while Ahmed was all alone. I had dragged Ramola into my problems and made her pay with her life. I was also afraid for Mark's life. I knew that if anything happened to Mark, I would never be able to forgive myself. I don't quite remember all the things that I told him that night; it was a jumble of all I was thinking.

I was terribly scared that Divakar would still be on the prowl. Mark told me, however, that Divakar had been silent for some time thanks to the coming elections. It was obvious that the party did not want to tarnish their name further by causing more public scandal. This reassured me a little. But there was something else I wanted to know. What had become of Ramola? I saw his eyes cloud when I asked after her. He kept avoiding that question, but I was persistent.

Mark held me close to his heart and spoke into my hair. 'Aradhana,' he said, 'I want you to be very brave. I have some very bad news. Ahmed has been arrested as the main suspect in Ramola's murder.'

I could not believe what I had just heard. It seemed even more impossible than all the horrific events I had witnessed. Mark gave me a newspaper. The front page had a banner headline: 'Muslim lawyer kills pregnant Hindu wife'. I did not bother to read the article. The ruling party was trying to conceal its connections with Divakar by making a communal issue out of Ramola's death. The whole scenario seemed infinitely bleak. I forgot my desire for freedom and personal happiness. The situation had become much bigger, beyond me. I felt tired of living and completely helpless. There seemed to be no law, no justice—no way of stopping Divakar from destroying all the people who had tried to help me and from finally getting to me and Tanya. In the process, who knew how many more innocent people would be hurt?

I looked at Mark in the blue glow of the bedside lamp. His brown eyes seemed almost black in that half-light. I reached for the only comfort and security I seemed to have in this world. When I awoke, I found myself still in his arms in the soft early morning sunlight that had silently replaced the shadows.

SIXTEEN

I told Mark that I had to give a statement to the police. I was the only eyewitness and I had to speak out. We went to the Chennai police headquarters and I asked to speak to the superintendent in charge.

We had to wait three hours before anyone came to speak to us. And even when he did, I don't think he considered what I said with any seriousness. He looked bored while I explained why I had come and glanced perfunctorily at my carefully-written account of the exact events that had occurred. He said that I should not interfere in police activity, and warned me to be careful and stay out of trouble. He refused to file an FIR based on it. A rush of blood filled my head. I walked out, knowing that they would toss my complaint into the bin.

Fortunately, there were other people fighting for Ahmed too. The Law Society was seething that a man famed for his crusade for justice had been so crudely framed. When I spoke to some of his friends there and told them that the police had refused to file an FIR, they were outraged. They knew that I was the only witness and asked me to speak to the press. I was initially petrified, but with their support, I knew I could do it. Besides, I could not let such a thing happen to Ahmed. I spoke to the chairman of the Law Society and declared my willingness to help. He agreed to organize a press conference in the union building.

The fact that I was going to narrate my version of events was in the evening papers and on TV. That evening, as I was sitting quietly in the balcony with Mark, I received a most unexpected telephone call. It was from my father. This was the first time I was talking to him since I left Darjeeling, and it felt like many lifetimes. He did not express any concern for Tanya or me, though. He merely asked me to stop what I was doing. He said that he had received threats about what would happen to him and my mother if I spoke up. For the sake of my mother, I should immediately come home and not involve myself in this sordid case.

It felt harder to stand up to him than all the other challenges I had faced. But I felt strangely liberated. I told him quietly that I had to do what I was doing and that I wanted him to support me in this. He hung up.

My father's telephone call made me realize anew how lucky I was to have Mark's unquestioning support. He never thought that there was any alternative to the course of action I had undertaken. I had to fight for Ramola and Ahmed because they had fought for me. And we could not let such injustice exist. It was as simple as that.

As I lay in Mark's arms that night, I thought of the

strange way in which events were unfolding and the bizarre twists my life had taken. All I had wanted to do was get out of a bad marriage, but because I had married an arrogant and wealthy man, matters had become complicated beyond belief. An innocent and brave woman had lost her life; her child had died without being born; I was alienated from my family forever—so many lives had been changed drastically and all for my own personal salvation from a life of continuing terror.

Before the press conference at the impressive Law Society building, I acknowledged with amazement that I was not nervous at all. I felt I owed it to Ramola. I said a prayer within my heart that my quest for justice would be successful. And then I took a deep breath and stepped out to address the crowded room full of journalists.

I tried to talk as factually and unemotionally as I could. I recounted all the events—from the time that we were kidnapped on that deserted road until I managed to get out early the next morning to summon help. There was a collective gasp when I pointed out that our assailants had addressed me by name and refrained from touching me, and that I recognized Ganapathi. There was total silence as I spoke. Finally, I took a deep breath and for the first time, brought up the subject of Divakar's connection with Vinay Kumar, which was the reason why the state government and police department were assisting him. I appealed to the collected journalists, representatives of free people and democracy, to ensure that justice was preserved and that an honest and upright man did not get unjustly punished.

Events moved rapidly after that. The revelations I

had made were in every newspaper, and made headlines on TV. The lawyers' union's demand that the complaint I had submitted at the police headquarters be registered as an FIR, was reinforced by public support. People took to the streets in a rally organized by the Law Society to protest against the miscarriage of justice. After about two weeks, the FIR was registered. I felt a glow of achievement when a copy of the FIR was finally sent to me as per police regulations. An arrest warrant was issued for Ganapathi. Finally galvanized into action, the Chennai police contacted the Darjeeling police. As Divakar's connection with Ganapathi had been mentioned in the FIR, Divakar was questioned at Darjeeling. A nation-wide hunt for Ganapathi was launched. He was found some days later in a little slum in Calicut. Along with him were two other men, whom I later identified as the men who had kidnapped us on that deserted beach road.

While the police investigation was in progress, matters on the political front were also changing. The elections were approaching, and the chief minister and his son did not want their names to be involved in a case where public sympathy was against them. The opposition parties were trying to get full political mileage out of the chief minister's unfair involvement in the Aradhana Divakar case, as the journalists referred to it. The state government would not risk the party's success over a single man. Thus, Divakar was no longer immune from the long arm of the law.

Finally things were moving, and I felt a sense of satisfaction that I might be able to secure some kind of justice for what had happened to Ramola. It all seemed quite futile now that Ramola was dead. But I felt the least I could do for that brave and vivacious woman who had befriended me in my hour of need, was to live according to her ideals and carry on her work, to try to emulate her own strength and conviction. I promised myself that I would continue the social work she had begun. The world had lost one strong woman. But I would do my utmost to be a living testimony to her ideals.

SEVENTEEN

When I awoke in the morning and went into the living room, the clock on the wall said eight. Mark was already up, reading the papers and sipping coffee. I instinctively started to apologize for sleeping late. Amma had trained me to be up at dawn, to make coffee for the men in the household. Mark kissed me good morning, and went to the kitchenette to pour me a mug.

He saw the guilty look on my face as he handed me the coffee, and squeezed my shoulders playfully. 'Aradhana, stop feeling guilty about me making you coffee. You can't feel guilty every morning for the rest of your life.' It was hard for me to overcome my years of training and accept that not only did he not mind that I was not making him his coffee, but that he was actually happy making it for me.

My life was settling into this peaceful rhythm which made me occasionally forget the horror that was lurking in the background. But as the weeks went by while we waited for the police investigation to be completed and the chargesheet submitted to the sessions court, it was easy to get lulled by the gentle winter weather, Mark's soothing presence and the simple pleasure of watching Tanya grow. However, it wasn't long before the outside world began pressing in again. It had been some three months since the police investigation began. Ahmed had called late last night to say that there were exciting developments and that he would be coming over in the afternoon to discuss them.

The only place I went to nowadays was Aurat Mandir. All through these months, I had carried on my work there. Some weeks ago, Renuka Tiwari called me to make me an offer I could not refuse. She wanted me to take up Ramola's position there. Of course I accepted the offer.

When Ahmed came over, he looked excited in a way I had not seen him look since before Ramola's death. He said that during the course of the police investigation, Ganapathi had decided to turn approver. He had named Divakar as the brain behind the whole operation and had identified his two accomplices on the day of Ramola's murder, as Ravi and Rajan. In the wake of this, Divakar had been arrested and denied bail. Ravi and Rajan were already in custody. The three of them had been cited as the accused in the chargesheet that had been submitted to the sessions court this morning.

We were all filled with a deep sense of thankfulness that matters were progressing as they should, and that the culprits would be punished for their heinous deeds. We sat on the balcony and discussed the implications of these developments. After a while, Ahmed asked me to go to Aurat Mandir with him. He had not been back there since Ramola died and as I drove there with him and Mark, I could not help remembering the day that Ramola had first taken me around the place.

We passed a vendor selling plants. I recognized a banyan sapling in his cart. I suddenly thought of my mother. Amma had told me that a woman should be like a banyan tree. She said that the banyan was very sacred for it always offered its branches to birds and gave weary travellers respite from the sun. 'Aradhana, when you grow up, I want you to be like the banyan.' I had nodded happily. I liked it when Amma told me such things. On an impulse, I told Ahmed to stop the car, and bought the sapling.

As the car drove into that serene campus, I felt a lump in my throat. Mark grasped my fingers firmly in his own. We got out of the car silently and walked into the office. There was a huge picture of Ramola there, adorned with a strand of jasmine. I stared at the picture for a long moment. I looked at Ahmed from the corner of my eye and I saw that he was gripping the table, his knuckles white against the dark rosewood surface.

We went out to meet the women and they crowded around us. I tried to tell them that I would try to take Ramola's place but the words got stuck in my throat.

One of the little girls piped up, 'Where is Ramola aunty? Why doesn't she come any more?' I picked up the little girl and held her close to me. 'You are Ramola,' I told her. 'Each one of us is Ramola. We should all be strong like her.' And it was true. Her death had given strength and resolution to all of us at Aurat Mandir.

Because she was not around to give us strength, we had all learnt to be strong in honour of her memory.

We went out and planted the sapling, and I told them some of the stories my mother had told me about the banyan tree. 'We women have to be like the banyan. We have to support and nurture all the people around us who need help,' I told them.

They looked at me in deep silence. They were all women who had suffered, but they all were instinctively caring and nurturing. I knew from their expressions that this ritual meant a lot to them.

When I went home, there were two very unexpected guests waiting for me—my parents perched primly at the edge of the sofa who looked totally stunned seeing Mark walk in with me. I could see their eyes travel beyond me and settle on him. Appa's face became stony and Amma looked down at the floor.

Mark extended his hand in friendly greeting and introduced himself. Muttering something under my breath, I escaped from the tense living room to the kitchen. Amma followed me.

'Aradhana, what is this? Is that man living with you?' She looked at me accusingly.

'Amma, he is visiting me.' I opened the kitchen cabinet and started to look for the coffee beans.

'Aradhana, come back with us. What is all this? You should not live here. Our reputation is gone. God, what is happening to our family!' She wrung her fingers anxiously.

I pretended to be very busy making coffee to avoid having to answer her. But Amma was adamant. She put her hands on my shoulders and turned me around to face her.

'Aradhana, Divakar is very upset. After all, you did have an affair.' She started to weep into the corner of her sari.

'Amma,' I said, my eyes wide with disbelief, 'are you really here on behalf of that murderer? Don't you believe in fighting for justice?'

'Aradhana, why this fighting and other things? Come and live with us. You are taking advice from Muslims and foreigners.'

I winced and started to respond angrily, but then I noticed her face. She looked so much older than when I had last seen her, and very tired. She saw me staring at her, and pointed to the red bindi on her forehead. 'Do you want me to lose this? Appa has been threatened so many times this week, you know.' She lowered her voice to a whisper. 'You should not appear in court for Appa's sake. The chief minister's personal lawyer met Appa. Appa has so much faith in you he has already promised that you will not go to court.'

She turned around as if the discussion was over and started to look in the refrigerator. I knew exactly what was going on in my mother's mind. When I was a child and there was a tense situation at home—usually between my father and his brother—Amma would start cooking. She would run into her kitchen as the argument became heated, to start chopping vegetables and marinating chicken. The sounds and smells of frying would fill the house. By the time she announced that the meal was ready, the argument would have died out. Appa would jovially serve the best pieces of chicken to his brother. So Amma believed that food—especially her cooking—could resolve all arguments. But unlike my father and his brother, I was not fighting about when the paddy field should be harvested or how much bonus the factory workers should get that year. I was fighting to secure justice for Ramola, and for all women, and this could not be resolved that easily.

I hated to hurt her but I had to. 'Amma,' I said, 'I am not going home, and I am going to court. Come outside and talk. Lakshmi will cook.' But she refused, so I asked Lakshmi to help her and went into the living room. Mark was playing with Tanya and Appa was scanning the papers.

'Well, Aradhana,' he said, 'I hope you will not be foolish enough to go to court.' He examined my face closely. Mark tactfully took Tanya out of the room to let us talk in private.

'Appa,' I said, 'I am going to testify against Divakar.'

'What about my word to the chief minister? I have promised him that you will behave.'

I looked at Appa and felt my temper rise. 'Appa, are you telling me to let a murderer get away?'

He said quite calmly, 'We decent people should not interfere in such things.'

I wanted to ask my father what he meant by 'such things', but I stopped myself. I knew I could never convince him.

The rest of the visit passed off quietly enough. When my father discovered that there was no point in trying to persuade me, he decided to go back to Madurai that very night. Amma agreed docilely. Before she left, she took me in her arms in the privacy of my bedroom. 'Aradhana,' she said, 'I want you to be safe. Promise me you will be careful.'

As I looked into her eyes, it suddenly dawned on me that in her heart, my mother believed that I was fighting for the right cause. A lifetime of believing in and living according to tradition prevented her from ever articulating this, but in her heart of hearts she believed in my ideals. Her eyes revealed that. She held me tightly to her, and I felt tears starting to slide down my cheeks. Her support meant more than that of the rest of the world put together. I felt as if I had found an ally, found my mother again. I felt rejuvenated.

'He seems to be a very nice man,' Amma continued against my shoulder. 'He will take care of you.'

I was stunned. I had not expected this. She smiled at the surprise in my eyes. The next minute we were laughing together. Beneath our laughter was a deep understanding. I hugged her tightly once more. It was hard to let her go.

After they had gone, I lay down thinking of my mother. I had always perceived her as the devout Hindu woman, upholder of traditions and culture, who believed in appeasing the gods with her penance. But now I wondered about her inner life as a woman. She had been married at twelve, so she had barely had a childhood. When I was that age, she had shown me a picture of herself as a bride, but she had not told me who it was. The little girl in the old Eastman colour picture looked small and frail with huge black kohl-painted eyes filled with trepidation. She wore a heavy, bejewelled sari. I gazed into the picture, thinking that it bore a striking resemblance to someone I knew. She looked almost like me!

'Aradhana, that was me at my wedding.'

I was shocked. I touched the picture; she looked even younger than her twelve years.

Amma had also shown me a little red blouse. The sleeves were so tiny! When I tried it on, it fit me a bit too snugly.

'That is my wedding blouse,' Amma said. 'It was a bit loose around the arms on my wedding day.' Her wedding bangles would not go past my wrists.

I had found it funny then, but now as I remembered, I started to cry. Poor Amma! She must have been absolutely terrified as a bride.

That day she had also shown me a photograph of herself when she was pregnant with Neela. She was barely thirteen and she had menstruated only once before she got pregnant. In the photographs, she looked like a frightened child with an incongruously large belly. She had become an adult, responsible for taking care of a child, when she was still a child herself. She must have been terrified of sex and childbirth, and on top of that, she had been criticized for giving birth to daughters.

I realized that all along I had not recognized that my mother was a person who had had individual dreams and hopes. She must have been very brave herself all her life. And now in her old age, she did not condemn me for violating every rule she had lived by, but reached out to encourage me, albeit silently. I waited for the day when I would see her again to share this new knowledge of her with her and to express my profound appreciation. My own strength had its origin in my mother. I had inherited her spirit after all.

EIGHTEEN

The day of the trial was set for May. Ahmed informed me that a very powerful lawyer called Arora had been hired to defend Divakar. I received a summons to be in court on 9 May 1997.

Mark drove me to the court and sat beside me. The courtroom was packed with reporters and the sweltering mid-summer heat was quite unbearable. When I saw Divakar's face across the room as he stood in the dock, I was filled with a sense of horror.

The public prosecutor handling this case was Salma Afridi, a highly respected woman of about thirty-five with a reputation for brilliance and honesty. She was nicknamed 'the Tigress' in legal circles. She had known Ramola, and I felt a sense of confidence that a woman who was obviously like Ramola in her integrity and intelligence was handling the case.

She started the proceedings by calling the witnesses for the prosecution to the stand. The first person called to present evidence was the forensic expert, Geet Kapur, who was asked to read out the autopsy report. In dry technical language, he explained that Ramola had died of strangulation and that she had been raped repeatedly before she died. The semen samples taken from her pubic area matched the DNA cultures taken from Ganapathi, Ravi and Rajan.

A chilled silence settled in the courtroom as this report was read.

Salma then called me to the stand to proceed with the evidence.

I felt strangely composed as I walked to the witness box. I swore on the holy book to speak the truth and nothing but the truth.

'Mrs Divakar, could you please tell me about the events of 17 September 1996?' Salma asked quietly.

'On 17 September 1996, I had arranged to meet Ramola at the Woodlands café. After we had finished, Ramola offered to drive me home. This was around two in the afternoon. We took the beach road and started to drive towards Besant Nagar. Midway, near a group of half-constructed flats, the car stalled. We tried to restart it but could not. We tried to flag down passing cars but none stopped. Finally, a scarlet jeep stopped. A man—Rajan—got out and pretended to examine our car. Then he and Ravi forced us to get into their car. Rajan addressed me as 'Mrs Divakar'. I was astounded when he called me that.'

The judge nodded her grey head as I said this.

I went on to describe what had happened, and by the time I finished my statement, I was nearly in tears.

'That's all, your honour,' Salma concluded.

The defence lawyer, Arora, rose ponderously to his feet to cross-examine me.

'Tell me, Mrs Divakar, why did you and the late Mrs Ahmed take the beach road to go to your apartment? Why did you not take the other less isolated roads?'

'It is a beautiful road, one which we frequently took. We were very happy and we wanted to enjoy the drive,' I said softly.

'Is it not strange that considering the fact that you were both involved in a controversial case, you still chose an isolated road?' he continued.

I knew that he was trying to focus on irrelevant details.

Salma noted it too and rose to her feet to object. 'Objection, your honour. The defence attorney is asking irrelevant questions to the witness.'

'Your honour,' Arora protested, 'this is relevant to the case.'

But he changed the track of his questions nevertheless. 'Mrs Divakar, you say that the men who assaulted and possibly killed Mrs Ahmed were Ganapathi, your husband's hired hand, and Ravi and Rajan. Where were you when the crime occurred?'

'I was in the same room.'

'Were you moving around freely in the room?'

'No, I was tied to a chair.'

'Was the room brightly lit, Mrs Divakar?'

'No, it was dimly lit.'

'So in the dim interior, when your friend was being raped, you took the time to observe Ganapathi's face?'

'I saw him clearly. He spoke to Ramola and me, so I also recognized his voice. It was Ganapathi,' I stated with conviction.

'That's right, Mrs Divakar. Ganapathi himself has admitted his crime. You were an eyewitness to the rape and the abduction, but you did not see the victim die.' He looked straight at me.

'That's correct,' I answered.

'So you were at the scene of the crime, and in a position to see and hear what was going on.'

'Yes.'

'Did you at any point hear Ganapathi or Ravi or Rajan refer to Divakar?'

'Well, they did not refer to him directly, but they addressed me as Mrs Divakar.'

'That is not proof. Of course you and this court are aware that Ganapathi did know you and that you knew him.'

I was silent.

'You have stated in your FIR that your husband, Divakar, hired Ganapathi to conduct the crime, and Ganapathi has also stated that your husband was paying him to do this. Now, Mrs Divakar, are you on good terms with your husband?'

'No.'

'Mrs Divakar, are you not currently living with a Canadian national, Mark Stratton?'

I was stunned by his question. Salma rushed to my rescue.

'Objection, your honour. The defence has no right to comment on the personal life of my client. He is defaming her in public and making a mockery of a murder trial. One woman has been raped and murdered, Mrs Divakar herself, abducted and terrorized. Mrs Divakar's personal life is of no concern to this court.'

'Your honour, my question is very relevant to the case. I think that Mrs Divakar, aided by Ganapathi, is trying to implicate Mr Divakar in the crime for her own interests. She is living with another man, and a husband can only be an inconvenience to her. That is what I am trying to establish. Therefore it is necessary for me to proceed with my line of interrogation.'

'Objection overruled. Mr Arora, you may proceed.'

'Thank you, your honour. Mrs Divakar, are you indeed having a relationship with Mark Stratton?'

I was silent.

'Mrs Divakar, perhaps Ganapathi spotted you in Chennai and raped your friend because of his own perverted desires. I would say that you are trying to implicate Divakar, and so you and Ganapathi have conspired to build up this false case against Mr Divakar, a man with an untarnished reputation. Your honour, I would like to tell this court that while the forensic report proves that Ganapathi, Ravi and Rajan did indeed rape the victim, there is nothing to prove that Divakar hired them to do the crime. Isn't that correct?'

'No,' I started hotly, and then faltered to a silence. Ganapathi had indeed called me Mrs Divakar and had carefully refrained from harming me, but there was no proof. I knew that Ganapathi had been acting under Divakar's commands, but how would we ever prove that?

NINETEEN

The trial progressed slowly as many witnesses for the prosecution were called and cross-examined. Slowly, the case against Divakar built up. Divakar himself seemed to realize that his position was very vulnerable. His lawyer, Arora, contacted Ahmed and requested that the matter be settled out of court. He also conveyed Divakar's offer that he would divorce me if I withdrew the charges. For a moment I was tempted—to be free of Divakar and this old life forever, to begin my life anew. But I knew I could never give up until I had avenged Ramola's death.

The truth needed no bargaining and the truth was my weapon. Secure in that conviction, I had a deep inner serenity which was fundamentally unaffected by all the problems besetting me. I loved my job at Aurat Mandir. I had never before been swathed with so much warmth and faith. I carefully watched the little banyan sapling grow. It grew stronger and more beautiful each day, the leaves unfurling with vigour, and the women at Aurat

Mandir tended it lovingly. I knew that just as one day that banyan would spread its strong branches and shelter a thousand birds, Aurat Mandir too, would reach out to many more women. That was my dream, and I worked quietly to do what I could to fulfil it.

Mark had to go to Darjeeling for an urgent two-day job. I needed him with me very badly; he was my only emotional support. I knew Amma was praying for my welfare and that her silent support was always there. But she was too far away. It was during those days that I comprehended fully how strong the other women at Aurat Mandir were. They gave me their company and support, and I realized how richly rewarded I was for the work I did.

It was while Mark was away that I had yet another unexpected visitor—my mother-in-law. I could not hide the shock in my eyes when I opened the door and saw her. I knew that she was Divakar's messenger. I let her in without a word. She sat on the couch and started to weep. I did not talk. She continued to sob loudly, cracking her knuckles and cursing all the gods who had wronged her. I looked away, unable to bear the drama, and reflected on the change in her. She was not her usual disdainful and arrogant self.

I remembered the first time I had met her, on the day before my wedding. I knew that much of my happiness in my husband's home would depend on her, and I had looked at her portly figure with fear and anticipation. She had come close to me and tilted my chin with a finger. 'What a pity that we have such a dark-skinned bride; I will have dark grandchildren.' Every time she had come to Darjeeling, she had tried to remedy that by insisting that I bathe with turmeric paste and fresh cream to lighten my skin. I hated the thick yellow paste, but she was always adamant and I had to comply meekly. Divakar demanded that her every word should be law.

I looked at her now, huddled and weeping, and she looked up pleadingly. 'Aradhana,' she said, clasping my hands in hers, 'Aradhana, please don't take away my son. I cannot live without him! Aradhana, please help the family! Our good name is your good name.' She started to sob again.

'I'm sorry,' I said. 'I cannot help you in this.' I got up and went to the window.

'Aradhana,' she said again, 'we'll do anything for you, only please let us be! We'll even give you your divorce. Just drop the charges. Don't spoil my son's life.'

'Your son has committed a murder,' I said as softly as I could. 'He has to be punished for that.' I felt sorry for her. It must have taken an enormous effort on her part— the all-powerful matriarch—to come begging at the door of an errant daughter-in-law. She left my house a disappointed woman. What a contrast she made to the domineering mother-in-law I was used to. I had seen her in her autocratic glory, and now it was her hour of defeat. She had enjoyed privileges for years because she had mothered a son; now she was facing the repercussions.

The trial continued with its many legalities and technicalities. There were many long gaps between hearings. It was like existing in a strangely suspended world.

The day Ganapathi finally gave his evidence as an

approver was a very difficult day for me. I had to look into the face of the man I had last seen when he was raping and murdering my friend. But his evidence clinched it. He stated that in August he had been paid a sum of two lakhs by Divakar, to come to Chennai and terrorize me in various ways. Also, he had been asked to get rid of Ramola—Ramola, the liberal, feminist, independent-thinking woman lawyer had been a thorn in Divakar's flesh—and in such a way, that I would be too intimidated to fight on any longer. He went on to describe how he had recruited Rajan and Ravi, and how the three of them had followed us around until the day they finally found us alone and vulnerable.

Arora rose to cross-examine Ganapathi while the court still sat in stunned silence, the only sound being the creaks of the ancient fans rotating above. 'Do you know Mr Divakar?'

'I have worked for him.'

'What kind of work do you do for him?' Arora asked.

'There are all kinds of odd jobs I do for him. When he needs anything sorted out.'

'Do you know Mrs Divakar?' There was a long silence. Ganapathi looked at me. I remembered the last time he had looked at me in that dimly-lit room.

'I have met her a couple of times in Darjeeling.'

'Ganapathi, you say that Divakar hired you to kill the victim. But didn't you have a grudge against him because of a dispute you had had over some money that you demanded? Isn't it because of this that you are trying to implicate him?'

Ganapathi did not answer.

Arora addressed the court. 'Your honour, my client Divakar tells me that Ganapathi had always been a troublesome employee and had lately been demanding large sums of money that were not due to him. When Divakar refused to pay him, he intended to kill Aradhana Divakar, but ended up killing Ramola. There are many precedents for this kind of murder where employees kill the family members of their employers for revenge.'

'Objection, your honour,' Salma was on her feet. 'Mr Arora is hypothesizing with no basis. He is trying to put the sole weight of the crime on Ganapathi. And his arguments are based on incorrect facts.'

'Objection sustained.'

'Your honour, my arguments are based on fact. I will be summoning Mr Sitaram, the accountant from Divakar's firm in Darjeeling, as one of the defence witnesses, and he will prove the accuracy of my statements.'

The case for the prosecution was wound up shortly after this, and soon after that, Mr Sitaram was summoned as a defence witness.

'Mr Sitaram,' Arora began, 'how long have you worked for Divakar?'

'Five years.'

'Do you know Ganapathi?'

'Yes, he has been working for Mr Divakar for longer than I have.'

'So you are quite close to him?'

'Yes, I have worked with him for five years.'

'Tell me, Mr Sitaram, what is your opinion of Ganapathi?'

'Ganapathi is the labour union leader and he was

creating a lot of politics in the company. Finally Mr Divakar had to bribe him to keep quiet. Mr Divakar phoned me one day and asked me to withdraw two lakh rupees and take it to Ganapathi's house. But even after this, Ganapathi was not satisfied. On 16 August 1996, Ganapathi contacted the boss and told him that the funds weren't sufficient and that he wanted a sum of five lakhs in total. When Mr Divakar refused, saying this was too much, Ganapathi resorted to threats.' Sitaram was perspiring heavily and kept mopping his brow with a large handkerchief.

'Did Mr Divakar speak to you about these threats?'

'Yes, he was very worried.'

'Your honour, from Mr Sitaram's testimony it is obvious that Ganapathi was not paid to do this crime, but that he did this crime because of greed for more money.'

Salma rose to cross-examine Sitaram.

'Sitaram, is Mr Divakar an unjust and cruel employer?'

'No,' Sitaram's thin bosom swelled as he launched into his defence of Divakar. 'Mr Divakar is the kindest of bosses. He pays large bonuses and takes care of all the employees and their families. In fact, in all the years that I have worked for him, there has never been a strike or any kind of unhappiness. There is always perfect love, we are like a fam . . .' Sitaram faltered into silence as he realized the import of what he had said.

'So, Mr Sitaram, there were no strikes, or threats of strikes, and the whole firm was like one family. That is what you were saying?'

Sitaram mopped his brow again. There was a long pause, at the end of which he said in a voice that was little more than a whisper, 'Yes.'

'In that case, I think that Mr Divakar would not have paid Ganapathi the sum of two lakhs for resolving labour problems if there was no labour problem, would he?'

Sitaram's voice could barely be heard as he mumbled, 'No.'

TWENTY

The trial dragged on, taking over our lives, shaping our days. When the court was not in session, we listlessly tried to get back to doing 'normal' things. The weight of evidence against Divakar mounted slowly but surely. The underhand nature of the 'work' that Ganapathi did for Divakar—extortion, blackmail and other similar activities—was slowly revealed. It was clear that Ganapathi would not have travelled without a purpose to Chennai and coincidentally found me with Ramola. It was also established that the money given to Ganapathi was not for resolving labour disputes, and that the amount he had spent to rent the house and secure the services of Ravi and Rajan could not have come from his otherwise limited resources.

Finally all the evidence for both the prosecution and defence was heard, and some two weeks later, the court heard the arguments of the prosecution and defence. The judgement would be given two weeks later.

The days seemed to drag interminably. It was August; the summer seemed endless and there was no sign of the monsoons arriving. Almost a year had gone by since that September day when I had met Ramola, radiant in the first months of her pregnancy.

When the day of judgement finally arrived, I realized that the events of this day would determine the course of the rest of my life. I sat in the deafening silence as the verdict was read out. Divakar, Ravi and Rajan were found guilty of the substantive offence under Sections 302 and 376, read with reference to Section 120-B of the Indian Penal Code. All three were sentenced to death by hanging.

I found myself hugging Ahmed and Mark. We had tears in our eyes. It seemed that we had achieved what had been the focus of our every waking moment for the past year. As we walked out of the Chennai sessions court, I held my head up high. The first monsoon clouds were gathering in the skies, as if to bring relief to the city after the torment of the summer, and the first raindrops were just beginning to fall. I looked up at the darkening skies and sent out a prayer for Ramola.

As we walked to where our car was parked, I saw Divakar being escorted to the white windowless van that would take him to his prison quarters. A thought flashed through my mind: the day some seven years ago when he had taken me as a new bride to Darjeeling, I had walked to what I had thought was my life sentence, just as he was walking today to his.

Ahmed, Mark and I went towards the car, but we wondered what to do. We felt somehow that we should celebrate, but there was no true joy in our hearts. Ramola's absence was always a tangible presence in our midst, but today it seemed stronger than ever. We knew we had to go to Aurat Mandir. We bought a sandalwood garland on the way. I held the sweet-smelling garland close to my face and the heady perfume seemed like a reminder of the good times ahead. Renuka was waiting at the gate to congratulate us. The women at Aurat Mandir gathered around us with smiles of joy. We walked to Ramola's picture in her office and put the garland around it. Her calm doe-like eyes seemed to congratulate me silently.

The voices of women were finally starting to be heard in our country. This was what Ramola had wanted. What had happened today showed that even a helpless woman could win a battle for justice; a reassuring reminder that good, coupled with courage, always has a way of winning.

That night as I lay with Mark, we finally got around to talking about our future. In all these months, life had seemed so uncertain that we had avoided raising this issue.

'Aradhana,' he said, his voice a whisper in my ear. 'I have to return to Canada very soon. Will you come with me?'

I wanted to go with him—that was my heart's fondest desire—but still I was silent. The only sound was the rain falling outside.

I looked into his eyes. 'Mark,' I said as gently as I could, 'what would happen to Aurat Mandir? I still have a lot of work to do there, you know. I cannot abandon those poor women. I am needed here for a while.'

Besides, I was still not free of Divakar legally. I

needed his signature to get a passport and visa for Tanya without which I could not go to Canada to be with Mark. I knew Mark had stayed back with me at considerable trouble to himself. He should have been back at work in Canada months ago. But he had not wanted to leave during the trial. All I wanted to do was to follow my heart and be with this wonderful man. But I knew that I had a responsibility to the memory of Ramola and to all women who suffered. There was a lot to be accomplished, and since I had been so lucky in my own life, I should reach out and try to help others.

I knew that Mark would understand my feelings and my reasoning. That was what was so miraculous about being with him: he had always supported my every decision, because it was mine and I was important to him. He was the rock that I had clung on to when I was drowning, and his faith and belief had made me strong enough to rebuild my life. I knew he was proud of the work I was doing at Aurat Mandir and would never ask me to leave it if I wanted to carry on.

'Aradhana,' he propped himself on his elbow and looked into my face. 'Aradhana, I love you, my darling.' He kissed me gently. 'I'll worry constantly about you, you know. I know that we will be together one day, but I want that day to arrive very soon. I want you beside me all the time.'

'Mark, that will happen one day. I will walk proudly by your side and never leave you again. But right now, I need to be here.'

We spent the night, weaving happy fantasies of the life we would live together one day.

The next few days passed quietly. It was bliss to know that the trial was finally over, and that Mark and I would always be together. At the same time, I knew that he would soon go back to Canada, and for some time at least, we would be apart. I tried to be brave about his departure.

When I thought about it, it still seemed amazing to me that I should have attained this kind of happiness and contentment. My parents brought me up to believe in established traditions and societal rituals. I grew up knowing that one day they would wrap me in silk and gold and hand me over to a man of their choice. But when only deep misery resulted from the marriage which had been arranged for me, I had been driven to desolation and despair. But somewhere, almost unknown to me, my dreams had lived on. I do not know what it was that made me fall in love with Mark. The most important thing was that I had learnt to trust another human being again.

The day Mark had to leave arrived with inevitability. I felt as if my heart would break as I watched him go. He was trying to keep his own emotions in check because we both recognized the need to be brave. We knew we would meet again, but it was still hard to say goodbye. As I watched him go through the glass door that separated the visitors from the travellers at the departure lounge at Chennai airport and turn to wave for the last time, I was hit by a wave of panic that seemed to swallow me.

When I reached home, the emptiness was overwhelming. I was overcome by an enormous listlessness. I sat in his favourite chair and began to dream of the time we would be together again.

In the days that followed, the newspapers were filled with articles about my case. Many people—known and unknown—called to congratulate me and say how inspired they were by my fight for justice. However, the people whose call would have meant the most to me, were silent. My father would never be able to relent enough to congratulate me on something he did not approve of. I am sure Amma was very happy, but she would never call me to say so.

The months went by swiftly. I was wrapped up in my work at Aurat Mandir. The institution was growing rapidly, and the publicity generated by the trial had brought us the much-needed volunteers and sponsors. We could now go ahead and implement many of the programmes that Ramola had held dear but had been unable to bring to fulfilment because of lack of resources. We started training programmes in tailoring, leatherwork and making pickles and preserves. We also started a school, for both the women and their children. Gradually we expanded these programmes so that destitute women from outside could also come in and learn. We helped the women to secure jobs so that they could leave the institution, become independent and have their own homes. Many of them came back to Aurat Mandir, to chat and to help out. Even when they had their own happy homes, they could not forget the strong sense of community we had shared at Aurat Mandir. The banyan sapling we had planted in the courtyard blossomed and grew into a resilient and beautiful young tree. My life seemed to have become like the waxing moon: every day it was reaching a greater level of strength and peace. Tanya turned two in April, and was every day a greater and greater joy to me.

I finally called my mother who was delighted to hear my voice, and she visited Tanya and me on Tanya's birthday. After she came on her own a couple of times— a new thing for her—my father started to accompany her. In spite of his disapproval of my actions, even he could not resist the charms of his only granddaughter!

The after-effects of the trial intruded occasionally into my life as Ahmed called me to inform me about what was happening. The High Court upheld the death sentence and the special leave petition to the Supreme Court by Divakar was dismissed. The President of India refused to grant pardon. At the state level, the ruling party had lost the elections by a big margin. Political analysts speculated that one of the reasons was probably the negative publicity generated by Ramola's murder.

Mark and I talked every day, and so strong was our sense of being together that even the physical distance seemed trivial. The only void was the one that was left behind by Ramola. I often thought of her incredible courage and confidence. I could never forgive myself that my leaving Divakar had indirectly been the cause of her death. But perhaps she would have wanted to be remembered as she was now seen all across the country— a martyr to the cause of the liberation of women in India. My story after all did not begin and end with me; it was merely a strand in the intricate fabric of the life of women in the country.

There was one morning when I woke up knowing

that this was the day Divakar was scheduled to die. It was strange but despite all the suffering he had put me through, I could still feel compassion for him. Behind that came the realization: today, finally, I was free of him.

Soon after this I began to feel restless. Aurat Mandir now had a large and competent staff, and all our programmes were running well. It was self-sufficient and I was no longer indispensable. My need to be with Mark grew stronger every day and the telephone calls were no longer enough.

In September, on the second anniversary of Ramola's death, Ahmed came to see me at Aurat Mandir, where he dropped in frequently in the evenings. He told me it made him very happy to see Ramola's dreams being fulfilled. As he looked across the lawn at the banyan tree, his face was filled with sadness. He turned and met my sympathetic look with a smile. 'You know, Aradhana, I have to be alone because the person I loved cannot be with me ever again. But you have someone you love and you should be with him. Life is short. You need to seize all the time you have to be together.'

It was a beautiful evening. The weather was beginning to cool down. But the world did not seem beautiful any more if Mark was not around. Suddenly, my mind was made up. I would go visit him.

Once my mind was made up, the rest fell into place smoothly. I left Tanya with my parents and packed my bags. I never enjoyed shopping more than when I was picking up all Mark's favourite things for him. I was excited, but at some level, also anxious. It had been over a year since I had seen him. Though I had talked to him every day, would things still be the same? I did not call and tell him I was coming; I wanted to surprise him. Though I was going to a faraway country and I had never been outside India, I did not feel intimidated. Going to Mark was like going home.

The flight to Toronto seemed interminable. As I sat in the confined space of the airline seat, my mind was filled with fear. Perhaps I was behaving too impulsively; perhaps we should have talked about this. The captain's voice assuring me that I was flying friendly skies did little to comfort me. I looked out of the window at the ocean of clouds, but even that tranquil sight did not soothe me.

When my flight landed at the Pearson International Airport in Toronto, it was evening and the wind was biting. I felt unusually calm as I completed the customs formalities and got my baggage together. I hailed a cab and asked the driver to take me to the nearest hotel.

I checked into the hotel wearily. I bathed and ordered some coffee. But the urge to see Mark overcame me. I dialled his number with nervous fingers and waited for him to pick up the phone. His 'hello' brought back that familiar feeling of comfort. At first, Mark thought that I was calling from India. It took him some time to register the fact that I was in Toronto. Before I knew it I was waiting for Mark to arrive.

When we finally saw each other again, it was like we had never been apart. So much had happened to me in my five years of marriage and over the past year. But it was as though every trial had only made me stronger. I felt the wholeness that comes with the freedom of choice.

And though I could never erase certain memories, I would always remember that I was blessed in many beautiful ways.